Surprises according to Humphrey

Betty G. Birney

PUFFIN BOOKS
An Imprint of Penguin Group (USA)

PUFFIN BOOKS
Published by the Penguin Group
Penguin Group (USA) LLC
375 Hudson Street
New York, New York 10014

USA * Canada * UK * Ireland * Australia
New Zealand * India * South Africa * China

penguin.com
A Penguin Random House Company

First published in the United States of America by G. P. Putnam's Sons,
an imprint of Penguin Young Readers Group, 2008
Published by Puffin Books, an imprint of Penguin Young Readers Group, 2009

THE LIBRARY OF CONGRESS HAS CATALOGED THE G. P. PUTNAM'S SONS EDITION AS FOLLOWS:
Birney, Betty G.
Surprises according to Humphrey / Betty G. Birney. p. cm.
Summary: While continuing to help his classmates solve their problems, Humphrey,
pet hamster of Longfellow School's Room 26, faces many surprises, like rolling
in a hamster ball, a substitute janitor who might be an alien,
and the possibility of Mrs. Brisbane retiring.
ISBN 978-0-399-24730-9 (hc)
[1. Hamsters—Fiction. 2. Schools—Fiction. 3. Interpersonal relations—Fiction.] I. Title.
PZ7.B5229Su 2008
[Fic]—dc22 2007007457

Puffin Books ISBN 978-0-14-241296-1

Printed in the United States of America

Designed by Katrina Damkoehler

19 20

To the GREATS—
Samantha and Carter Radman
Rita and Josie de Leeuw
and Ethan Birney.

Contents

Spring Has Sprung

Monday mornings are different than other mornings. That's just one of many things I've learned in the months I've lived in Room 26 of Longfellow School.

For one thing, on Mondays, I'm usually tired from a weekend spent visiting the home of one of my fellow classmates. That's the BEST-BEST-BEST part of my job as classroom hamster.

My friends are also quieter than usual on Mondays. It takes them at least half a day to get back up to speed after their weekends away from school.

Don't-Complain-Mandy Payne complains more than usual on Mondays. Today, she complained that it was too hot. Our teacher, Mrs. Brisbane, opened a window.

Sit-Still-Seth Stevenson jitters in his seat more on Monday mornings. But he tries to sit still; he really does.

And even Lower-Your-Voice-A.J. Thomas, who can rattle the walls with his loud voice, is quieter on Monday mornings. It's weird.

Mrs. Brisbane, however, is always up to speed, and she likes to get Monday mornings rolling with something interesting.

"Class, in case you hadn't noticed, spring has sprung!" Mrs. Brisbane announced one Monday.

I don't know about the other students, but I'd certainly noticed that the March rains had stopped and everything had changed. The world, which had been drippy and dreary, was now bright green. The trees, the grass—just about everything outside—matched the color of my goofy green neighbor, Og the Frog, who lives in a tank next to my cage.

For some reason, all that green made me feel like springing up onto my bridge ladder, which goes across my big cage.

Mrs. Brisbane kept talking. "Today, I have a special spring surprise for you!"

Surprise? Surprises are fun, like birthday presents. But surprises can be not so fun, like unexpected storms with LOUD-LOUD-LOUD thunder that can hurt the ears of small, sensitive creatures like me. Just thinking about thunder made me bobble, then wobble. I tried to catch my balance but tumbled off my ladder with a loud *thump!* Luckily, I landed in a pile of soft bedding (and not in my poo corner), but still, I was very surprised and quite startled.

My neighbor, Og, was startled, too, I guess, because he let out a large "BOING," which is the strange twanging sound that green frogs, like him, usually make.

"What's going on over here?" Mrs. Brisbane walked toward the table by the window where Og and I live.

"Humphrey fell! I saw him!" a voice called out. Even

though I couldn't see who was talking from underneath all that bedding, I knew it was Raise-Your-Hand-Heidi Hopper, because no matter how many times she'd been told, Heidi never remembered to raise her hand.

"Hands, please, Heidi," Mrs. Brisbane reminded her.

I poked my head out of the bedding and saw her looking down at me. "Are you all right, Humphrey?"

"I'm not hurt," I explained. "But I am a little shaken up."

As usual, all that came out was, "SQUEAK-SQUEAK-SQUEAK."

"He certainly sounds fine," said Mrs. Brisbane. "Now, back to our surprise."

I stood up to give her my full attention.

"I've been working you pretty hard on our pre-test drills," she continued.

That was certainly true. We had tests from time to time in Room 26. But there were *bigger* tests coming, and Mrs. Brisbane wanted to make sure her students did well. There were math drills and reading drills and her favorite: the dictionary drill. Every day, she had a list of words for us to look up in the dictionary. Then we were supposed to write sentences using the words correctly.

There was just one problem: everyone in class had a dictionary except me! This was very annoying, because I try to keep up with my friends. Finally, I came up with a solution and made my own dictionary by writing words and definitions in the tiny notebook I keep hidden in my cage. Ms. Mac, the wonderful substitute teacher who brought me to Room 26, gave it to me. (She also gave me a broken heart when she left to teach in far-away Brazil. I still think about Ms. Mac a lot.)

Now Mrs. Brisbane was smiling broadly. "This morning, we're taking a break from drills to decorate the room."

My classmates cheered.

"What did she say?" Pay-Attention-Art Patel asked Lower-Your-Voice-A.J.

"No test drills!" A.J. bellowed loudly.

That got Stop-Giggling-Gail Morgenstern chuckling and her best friend, Heidi, joined in.

Mrs. Brisbane shushed everyone. "Settle down. The theme of the day is Spring into Numbers. Now, let's get to work!"

None of us knew what she was talking about, but soon, all my friends were busy with paper, paint, markers, fluffy cotton, string and wire. How I wished I could get my paws on some of those things!

While Mrs. Brisbane explained that the students were supposed to hide math problems in their flower, tree and kite projects, I scurried to my wheel for a little exercise. Spring made me feel frisky and full of life! I spun faster and faster until the whole room was a blur. And then the recess bell rang.

My classmates dropped their markers and construction paper and raced toward the door. Wait-for-the-Bell-Garth Tugwell was the first one out, as usual.

For some reason, the bell surprised me, maybe

because it sounded a little softer than normal. I guess it surprised Mrs. Brisbane, too, because she glanced at the clock and shouted, "Children! Come back here!" She raced to the door and called the students back. "It's not recess yet."

I could hear them objecting.

"It was the bell!" A.J. bellowed.

"We'll miss recess!" Mandy protested.

But Mrs. Brisbane was firm. Once my friends were back in the room, she pointed to the clock. "See? It's not time yet." She checked her watch. "Not for another half an hour."

"But the bell rang!" Heidi argued.

"Raise-Your-Hand-Heidi," Mrs. Brisbane said, just as she's said hundreds of times before. "Would someone like to tell me what just happened?" Mrs. Brisbane's eagle eyes stared out at the classroom.

"April fool!" a voice called out.

"I-Heard-That-Kirk Chen," the teacher said. "It was you, wasn't it?"

Kirk was the class comic, but he'd been better lately about pulling practical jokes during school hours.

"I'm sorry, Mrs. Brisbane," Kirk answered. "But it's April first. April Fools' Day! You're supposed to play jokes on people."

Mrs. Brisbane asked him to explain what he did.

"Last week, I made a recording of the recess bell." He held up a TINY-TINY-TINY tape recorder. "I just played it a little ahead of time."

Mrs. Brisbane shook her head. "Kirk, I don't know what I'm going to do with you."

"I didn't hurt anybody," Kirk protested.

"No, but—"

Mrs. Brisbane didn't finish because all of a sudden the loudest sound I've ever heard rattled my furry little ears. It was much louder than the buzzers and bells that sound at morning, recess, lunchtime or at the end of the day. It was louder than the loudest voice A.J. ever used. It wasn't a ringing or a buzzing—it was an earsplitting BEEP-BEEP-BEEP without stopping.

"Help!" I squeaked, plummeting off my wheel and somersaulting through my bedding. It's never a good idea to stop spinning too quickly.

"Fire drill!" Heidi called out. She didn't raise her hand, but this time, Mrs. Brisbane didn't scold her.

The beeps kept blaring. Couldn't someone turn them off?

"Boys and girls, it *is* the fire alarm," Mrs. Brisbane shouted. "Leave everything on your desks. Line up row by row and we'll calmly walk out to the playground."

"BOING-BOING!" Og sounded worried.

We hadn't had a fire drill since Og came to our classroom. No wonder he was alarmed. I quickly explained that a fire drill is a time for students to practice how to act if there's a fire. My friends knew just what to do. They put down their pencils, scissors and papers, stood up and began to form lines.

"Stay calm," Mrs. Brisbane said. I don't know how

6

anyone could stay calm with that noise. "They didn't tell me about a fire drill, so this one could be a real alarm."

I was impressed with how orderly the students were, except for Miranda Golden, who was usually one of the best-behaved students in class. She left the line and hurried to my cage. "Come on, Humphrey. I'll look out for you."

Good old Miranda. I think of her as Golden-Miranda, because she is an almost perfect person. And her hair is as golden as my fur.

Then Garth and A.J. broke ranks and raced over to Og. Each of them took one end of his tank to carry him.

"Children! Stop!" Mrs. Brisbane shouted. "Leave Og and Humphrey here. You must leave everything in the classroom!"

"But if it's a real fire, we can't leave them here!" Miranda protested. I do love that girl.

"Yeah, that would be awful!" A.J. agreed.

Mrs. Brisbane bit her lip and looked out into the hallway. "It's probably a surprise drill, but all right. Hurry along. And keep that tank level, please!"

I didn't know if there was a fire or not, but it felt like we were having an earthquake, because as Miranda carried my cage, I was slipping and sliding. Thank goodness for that nice, soft bedding!

As my cage lurched down the hall, I saw us head toward a side door. This was a surprise because I'd only been in and out of the school through the front door before. Suddenly, I felt fresh spring air on my fur and there was BRIGHT-BRIGHT-BRIGHT light in my eyes. I couldn't smell any smoke, and best of all, the awful beeping stopped.

"It's okay, Humphrey," Miranda told me. "We're out on the playground."

The playground? The playground! The place where my classmates went every day but where I had never been before. I took a chance and stood up to look around. I saw swings, a slide, a tall something-or-other with rings hanging down from it. It was almost as cool as my cage with its wheel, ladders and tree branches.

And there were students and teachers from other classes standing around. There was Small-Paul Fletcher, who was in Mrs. Loomis's class but came into Room 26 for math every morning. He didn't look so small compared to the other students in his class.

Wow, I'd never seen that tall teacher with the bright red hair. Or the teacher who looked a little bit like Santa Claus. They were all talking and laughing, so I knew it was just a practice fire after all. I was still taking it all in when—SCREECH!—the loudest whistle on earth blasted very near my cage.

"Mrs. Brisbane!" a voice bellowed.

A shadow fell over my cage. I looked up and saw that the large object casting the shadow was actually a woman. A woman holding a whistle.

"You should know by now that nothing should be taken from the classroom. Nothing!" Her voice was almost as loud as her whistle, but a lot deeper.

"I know, Mrs. Wright, but the children had a point. If this was a real fire, they would want to save their pets."

"Unacceptable!" the woman called Mrs. Wright declared. I braced myself in case she blew her whistle again.

"He's a living creature! A living thing!" said Miranda. Did I mention how much I love that girl?

Then I heard a familiar voice. "What's going on here?"

"A serious breach of the rules," Mrs. Wright roared. "Nothing must leave the classrooms except the students. Nothing!"

"And the teacher!" I added. I was a little afraid of this woman, but still, someone had to squeak up for Mrs. Brisbane.

I saw Mr. Morales's face smiling down at me. He's the principal and also the Most Important Person at Longfellow School. As usual, he was wearing an interesting tie. This one had fluffy white clouds on a blue background.

"You mean Humphrey? And Og?" he asked.

"They're not things, Mr. Morales. They're living creatures," Miranda protested.

"And they're part of our class," added Garth.

"Yeah!" A.J. bellowed, and this time Mrs. Brisbane didn't tell him to lower his voice.

Mrs. Wright waved a paper in Mr. Morales's face, which was RUDE-RUDE-RUDE!

9

"There are rules, and as Supervisor of Emergency Services, I must strongly protest," she said. "I'm sorry, but Mrs. Brisbane has chosen to ignore the rules!"

Those were fighting words. Because nobody I knew followed the rules better than Mrs. Brisbane. At least if they were good rules.

"Look, the children have a point," she said, in a nice, soft voice (unlike Mrs. Wright's loud, unpleasant voice). "You can't expect them to leave behind their beloved pets."

"It's up to us to enforce the rules." Mrs. Wright fingered her whistle, but thank goodness, she didn't blow on it.

"Well . . . ," said Mr. Morales.

"If I had argued with them, it would have slowed us down," Mrs. Brisbane explained. "That's not good in a fire."

"BOING!" Goodness, I was surprised to hear Og squeak up, but I was glad he was on our side.

Then I heard a brand-new voice. "That went well," a man's voice said.

Mrs. Wright shook her head. "Not entirely. We'll have to try again before the end of the year."

The person behind the new voice came into view. He was wearing a big shiny yellow jacket and big yellow pants. And on his head was a COOL-COOL-COOL black hat with a big brim and a red 29 on it.

"Hi, folks," he said, smiling. "I'm Jeff Herman from Engine Company Twenty-nine."

"Did you bring the fire truck?" Garth asked.

"It's out front. You guys did a good job with the fire drill today."

Mrs. Wright shook her head. "I'm afraid these children did not. They took the time to bring this rat and this frog outside. Strictly against the rules."

A rat! I would think that a person who teaches school could tell the difference between an ordinary rat and a handsome golden hamster, like me!

Firefighter Jeff pushed his hat back on his head. "If there's a real fire, you shouldn't stop to get your pets. Your job is to get out safely. Don't go back in for anything. But tell the firefighters your pet is inside. We rescue pets from fires all the time."

He bent down and looked me right in the eyes. "Especially nice little hamsters like this guy."

At least one smart person could tell a hamster from a rat!

"But the best thing to learn is how to prevent a fire from happening," he continued. "I'll tell you about that when I visit your class later."

WOW-WOW-WOW! A real, live firefighter was coming to Room 26! Now, *that's* the kind of surprise I like.

DICTIONARY: A book giving the meanings of very cool words, how to say them and where those words came from. (Question: Is the word *dictionary* in the dictionary?)

Humphrey's Dictionary of Wonderful Words

Stop, Drop and More Surprises

Kirk had to stay in during afternoon recess and write a letter of apology on the chalkboard.

Even though she acted angry, I don't think Mrs. Brisbane thought his prank was that bad. After all, it was very clever of him to think of recording the bell.

True to his word, Jeff Herman stopped by our classroom late in the day. He showed us pictures of very cool fire engines with noisy sirens, and he told us not to play with matches (which I've never done). He said that if you are in a building that's on fire, you should "stay low and go." That means you should stay low to the ground and get out of the building. Then he told us something very important: if your clothes ever catch on fire, you should remember three things.

"Who knows what those three things are?" he asked.

Seth and Garth raised their hands right away, but before anyone called on them, Heidi blurted out, "Stop, drop and roll!"

"Raise-Your-Hand-Heidi Hopper. *Please!*" Mrs. Brisbane sounded really annoyed. "Sorry, Mr. Herman," she told the firefighter.

He just smiled and explained that if you or a friend ever have your clothes catch on fire, you should stop, drop to the floor and roll. That will put out the fire. Then came the fun part. He made us all practice. My friends stood by their desks (and I stood in my cage) and shouted, "Stop! Drop! Roll!" Then we'd drop to the ground and roll on the floor. I was luckier than my friends because I have such soft bedding on the bottom of my cage. I think even Og must have practiced because I heard splashing coming from his cage.

Jeff Herman gave the students stickers that said Stop-Drop-Roll, and suddenly, school was over for the day. Everybody was smiling and happy except for Mrs. Brisbane. She frowned as she stopped Heidi on her way out of class.

"Heidi, it's bad enough when you won't raise your hand in class, but when we have a guest and you speak out like that, it's rude and embarrassing."

Heidi looked up at Mrs. Brisbane with big sad eyes. "I'm sorry," she said. "I forgot."

"You remember to come to school and you remember to do your homework, I'm happy to say. Why can't you remember to raise your hand?"

"I guess it's a bad habit," Heidi explained.

Mrs. Brisbane sighed loudly. "I'd better call your parents in. Again."

The Hoppers had already been in twice this school

year, and both times they said Heidi was well behaved at home. They promised to talk to her about her disruptive behavior. Each time, Heidi was quiet for a day or two after the meeting, but she'd always gone back to blurting things out.

Mrs. Brisbane dismissed Heidi so she could catch her bus. Then she slowly walked over to the table where Og and I live.

"Fellows," she said, "if there's one thing I want to accomplish by the end of the school year, it's getting Heidi Hopper to raise her hand."

"If anyone can do it, you can!" I shouted, but of course, all she heard was "SQUEAK-SQUEAK-SQUEAK." That's the problem with being a classroom hamster. I can read, I can write and I can help my friends. But it's hard for me to make myself understood.

"Sometimes I wish I had a magic wand to wave all my students' problems away," she said. Then she stared right at me. "Come to think of it, Humphrey, you're not too good about raising your paw, either. See you boys tomorrow."

After she left, I thought about what Mrs. Brisbane had said. "You know, Og, I understand Heidi's problem," I told my neighbor. "I do forget to raise my paw before squeaking up in class. Of course, I wouldn't get called on anyway. But Heidi could, and she's a smart girl. She should be able to learn."

"BOING!"

I'd finally decided that the odd sound Og made was his way of agreeing with me. "And Mrs. Brisbane knows so many things, like how to get Speak-Up-Sayeh to speak up and how to get Pay-Attention-Art to pay more attention. Surely she can find a way to help Heidi."

Og apparently didn't have any opinion on the subject, so I crawled into my sleeping hut to think things over.

•~•~•

SQUEAK-SQUEAK-SQUEAK. The sound woke me from my doze, and this time I wasn't the one squeaking. It was Aldo Amato, coming in to clean the room. His cart needed a little bit of oil to stop that noise.

I peeked out from my sleeping hut. The lights came on, temporarily blinding me, but I heard Aldo's familiar voice.

"¡Buenas noches, señores! ¿Cómo estás?"

The voice sounded like Aldo's, but for the first time ever, I couldn't understand a word he was saying. It reminded me of the weekend I spent at Sayeh's house, when I couldn't understand her family. It took me a while to realize that they were speaking another language. But Aldo had always spoken English until tonight.

"Aldo? Is that you?" I squeaked.

My eyes got used to the light, and I could see that the person in the room actually was Aldo. He stopped and looked up at the clock. *"Son las siete y medio."*

"Huh?" I squeaked.

15

Og let out an alarmed "BOING!" I guess he was surprised to hear Aldo's strange new way of speaking, too.

Aldo looked puzzled. "Or is it *media*? I always forget." He set to work, moving the desks, sweeping the floor, dusting the desks, all the while muttering strange words, like, *"Me llama Aldo. ¿Cómo está usted? ¿Dónde está el . . . ? ¿Dónde está la—*oh, *mamma mia,* those *el*s and *la*s. *¿Dónde está la escuela?"*

He swept more and more furiously.

"Tengo un lápiz. Él tiene un lápiz. Tienen . . . tienen . . . lápices."

"Og, can you understand what he's saying?" I called over to my green, googly-eyed friend.

"BOING-BOING!" he twanged back.

Yep, he was just as puzzled as I was.

Aldo put the desks back in place, then pulled up a chair close to my cage and took out his lunch bag. He tore a little piece of lettuce from his sandwich and poked it through the bars of my cage. "Here, *muchacho.*"

"Thanks!" I squeaked.

"I don't know the word for *lettuce.*" Aldo sounded discouraged.

What on earth was my friend talking about? The word for *lettuce* is *lettuce,* isn't it?

Aldo ate in silence, then suddenly stood up. "Well, gotta go, *amigos,"* he said, opening the blinds.

Sometimes Principal Morales calls me *amigo,* so it must be something good.

"¡Hasta luego!"

I never heard *that* before. "Whatever," I squeaked back in total confusion.

Soon, Aldo was gone, the lights were out and the room was bathed in the silvery glow of the streetlight. I could hear Og swimming in his tank, but I didn't pay much attention.

I was too busy thinking about Aldo and wondering what was wrong with him. He and I had always understood each other pretty well . . . until tonight.

Night is a funny time. It's the time when most of us hamsters are usually active. And it's the time when most humans are sleepy. It's a good time for thinking, but sometimes thinking can turn to worrying, at least for me.

I wasn't just worried because I couldn't understand Aldo. I was also worried about what would happen if the fire alarm started beeping at night. Who would carry Og and me outside? At least I knew how to STOP-DROP-ROLL, thanks to that nice firefighter, Jeff.

Then I remembered my lock-that-doesn't-lock. While it appeared to be locked to humans, I could open it and come and go as I pleased. So, in case of a fire, I could escape if I had to. That was a relief. But what about Og? Then I remembered that he had popped the top off his tank a few times before. Somehow, I knew that Og and I would scurry, hurry and hop our way to safety.

Once I figured that out, I felt a LOT-LOT-LOT better, and the next thing I knew, the morning bell was ringing and another day of school was about to begin.

SURPRISE: Something totally unexpected and unplanned for. A surprise can be good, like a postcard from Ms. Mac. Or a surprise can be bad, like Ms. Mac moving to Brazil. A surprise can also be both good and bad, like a shiny balloon (a good thing) that suddenly pops and scares you (a bad thing).

Humphrey's Dictionary of Wonderful Words

Hamster on a Roll

I learned a lot about human behavior during my first seven months in Room 26. Humans can be funny, sad, happy and mad . . . all in one day! But the one person I can't quite understand is Mrs. Brisbane. Just when I think I have her figured out, she does something she's never ever done before.

For instance, every single morning, she comes into the classroom, puts her books on her desk and her purse in the desk drawer, checks her hair in the mirror, then walks toward the window and says, "Good morning, fellows. Here's hoping for another great day!"

I always tell her that I'm sure it will be unsqueakably great, and Og sometimes answers with his goofy "BOING!"

But on Tuesday, for the first time all year, she came into the room, dumped her books on the desk, put her purse in the drawer and slammed it shut. Then she walked over to the bulletin board and stared at the cutouts of the planets that were up there. "I wonder how many bulletin boards I've put up and taken down over the years?" she asked.

I hoped she wasn't asking me because I didn't have an exact answer. I did know that Mrs. Brisbane had been teaching for many years, so the answer would be LOTS-LOTS-LOTS.

She shook her head and began taking down the cutout pictures of planets with interesting names like Neptune, Jupiter and Saturn.

Then there was Mars, which is an angry-looking red color, with spots on it that look like big scary eyes, especially at night. I wasn't sorry to see that picture go.

The bulletin board was empty by the time the students started streaming in. For months, they'd come in bundled up in coats and boots, hats and gloves. Now they had on light jackets and sweaters, and it didn't take long for them to hang their things in the cloakroom and hurry to their seats.

I-Heard-That-Kirk came bounding into the room with a big smile on his face.

"Mrs. Brisbane, I'm sorry about yesterday. To make up for it, I have a surprise for Humphrey. Can I give it to him now?" he asked.

A surprise for *me*? That got my whiskers wiggling.

And it started Gail giggling. "What is it?" she said. "Let me see!"

Soon, the other students were gathered around Kirk, begging him to let them see the surprise.

"Okay, Kirk. What is it?" asked Mrs. Brisbane. Her arms were folded, and she had a suspicious look on her face. After all, Kirk had done a few things that would make any teacher unhappy. Once, he put a cushion on Repeat-It-Please-Richie's chair that made a VERY-VERY-VERY rude noise when Richie sat on it. He called it a "whoopee" cushion. My friends laughed so hard (including Richie), they all wanted a chance to sit on it, but Mrs. Brisbane took it away and made Kirk sit in the cloakroom for a while.

This time, Mrs. Brisbane held out her hand. "Let me see it, Kirk," she said. Boy, she sure didn't trust him.

Kirk reached in his backpack and pulled out something I couldn't see. All of my friends went "ooh" and "aah," which made my heart thump faster and faster.

"Can you see it, Og?" I squeaked to my tablemate.

There was no answer.

"It's a hamster ball. We can put Humphrey inside, and he can roll around the classroom. See, there are air holes in it. It's good exercise," Kirk explained. "Can we try it?"

The thought of rolling around the classroom during the day was so exciting, I climbed up on my ladder to get a closer look.

Mrs. Brisbane held the clear yellow ball in her hand. "Well," she said. "I suppose it would be nice for Humphrey. But we have to be careful that we don't step on him or that he doesn't roll someplace dangerous."

My friends all cheered, and I joined in. Og started splashing, so I knew he approved.

"*And,* we can't let this interfere with our schoolwork. Testing is coming up, you know," Mrs. Brisbane said with a frown.

Kirk had already opened my cage.

"Don't hurt him," said Golden-Miranda, who's always looking out for me.

Kirk placed me in the ball, then snapped the top shut.

"Make sure it's closed tightly, please," Speak-Up-Sayeh said softly. She was shy, but she always looked out for me, too.

It was kind of weird being enclosed in a round object. Since it was yellow plastic, the world looked yellow to me, and Miranda was more golden than ever. I checked to see that there were holes in the plastic. YES-YES-YES! I wouldn't have trouble breathing.

"Careful now," warned Mrs. Brisbane as Kirk set the ball on the floor at the front of the classroom.

My fellow students crouched down to watch.

"Go on, Humphrey Dumpty," said A.J. "Make the ball go."

Let me tell you, it's very strange to be inside a ball. For one thing, there's nothing flat to stand on, like a floor. So even standing still, the ball felt wobbly.

"Run, Humphrey," said Seth. "Get it moving!"

I hesitated for a little bit, but when I heard Og go "BOING!" I knew I had to move.

I went slowly at first, just taking tiny steps. My friends moved back to give me room to roll down the center aisle.

"Go, Humphrey, go!" said Kirk.

I jogged a little faster.

"Go, Humphrey, go!" the other students chanted. "Go, go, go!"

I liked the encouragement and I liked the feeling of going fast, so I began to run. It was like spinning my wheel, only this time, I was actually going somewhere!

Many times before, I'd scurried across the floor of the classroom, but never when the other students were there. As I zoomed down the aisle between the tables and chairs, my friends followed me.

The bell rang, which meant school had begun, but once I got rolling, I didn't know how to stop. As much fun as the hamster ball was, it was SCARY-SCARY-SCARY, too, because I couldn't control where I was going.

I heard Mrs. Brisbane say, "Class, we need to begin our work!" But I was on a roll, heading right for—eek!—the wall!

Someone gasped. I think it was Miranda. "He'll crash!" she said. "Stop him!"

I tried to slow down, but it was too late. The ball bounced off the wall and shot back toward the aisle. I was now upside down, and before I could get back on my feet, I came to a stop that was so sudden, I did a double flip inside the ball. I looked up and saw a large foot in a sensible black shoe.

It was Mrs. Brisbane's foot.

"Class, I want you all in your seats. Take out a sheet

of paper for the dictionary drill. I'll take attendance while you get started."

I was catching my breath when she leaned down over me. "And you, young man, will settle down."

When Mrs. Brisbane talks like that, nobody argues with her, especially not a small golden hamster enclosed in a ball. Once she removed her foot, I cautiously headed back down the center aisle between the desks.

Mrs. Brisbane kept a close eye on me while my friends took the test. Usually, I took the test along with them, writing the answers in my notebook. But I was enjoying my freedom a little too much for that. I kept on jogging up and down the center aisle, but now, I was careful to slow to a stop before hitting a wall. That way, I just tapped it, rolled backward, then turned my body inside the ball and jogged toward the opposite wall again.

My friends wrote quietly while Mrs. Brisbane gave out the words. I tried not to make too much noise as I sailed past Mandy's shiny red shoes, Art's black high-tops and Garth's scuffed white sneakers. Sit-Still-Seth's feet TAP-TAP-TAPPED as he wrote.

I don't know how many times I went back and forth, but it was getting a little boring. If only I could turn the thing! After the test papers were collected, Mrs. Brisbane said it was time to finish the Spring into Numbers project. I think my friends forgot about me while they cut and pasted, colored and stapled their papers.

By recess time, Room 26 looked completely different.

The bulletin board was covered with cutouts of flowers, rabbits and robins—but they all had math problems on them. Plus and minus numbers, multiplying and dividing problems peeked out from the leaves of the blossoms and ran up and down the rabbit ears and robin wings.

Tabitha and Richie made clouds in all kinds of shapes—even triangles and squares. Gail and Sayeh tacked a row of colorful flowers all around the chalkboard. There was a pattern to the colors, and it took me a while to figure it out. Garth and A.J. made a huge kite with a LONG-LONG-LONG tail that had a LONG-LONG-LONG problem on it.

I began to jog with joy. Spring was bright! Spring was happy! Spring was fun!

While Mrs. Brisbane helped hang the kite, I suddenly hit the leg of Seth's desk and veered off toward the door, which was open to let in the spring breeze.

I sailed out of Room 26, and not one of my friends noticed.

"HELP-HELP-HELP!" I squeaked. In the distance, I heard Og's "BOING!" but everything was completely silent in the hall. As I rolled out of Room 26, toward the side door, I wondered if I'd end up on the playground again. I frantically tried to guide the ball away from the door, but it wouldn't turn quickly enough.

Luckily, the door was closed tightly, so I bounced off of it. Now I was heading toward another door. It was FAR-FAR-FAR away, past a long row of classrooms. Suddenly, I wished Aldo hadn't polished the floor quite so well. I also wished the hamster ball had brakes. The best I could do to slow it down was to stop moving my legs.

What an unsqueakably dangerous situation for a small hamster! At least my cage had that lock-that-doesn't-lock. But there was no way for me to get out of the ball.

"Good-bye, Room 26!" I squeaked.

Suddenly I heard a piercingly loud noise. (Hamsters are very sensitive creatures, and we don't appreciate loud noises.)

"Stop right there," a voice firmly ordered me. The ball stopped abruptly, and this time I did a triple flip. But I recognized the voice . . . and the shrill sound. It was Mrs. Wright and her whistle. She was standing directly in front of me with one of her huge, white, puffy shoes resting on top of the ball.

Just for fun, I guess, she blew her whistle again.

"Mrs. Brisbane!" she bellowed.

Mrs. Brisbane rushed out into the hallway and hurried toward us. "What's wrong, Mrs. Wright?"

That sounded funny, but I wasn't in the mood to laugh. I was afraid Mrs. Wright might blow her whistle again.

"I just happened to be coming down the hall when I found your *rat* out here!"

"For goodness' sake." Mrs. Brisbane leaned down and picked up the ball. "How did you get out here?"

"You created a very dangerous situation," said Mrs. Wright. "Someone could trip over him and get hurt."

"Well, no one did," said Mrs. Brisbane. "Don't worry, it won't happen again."

Mrs. Wright sniffed loudly. "Still, I must report this to Mr. Morales."

"Do whatever you think you should." Mrs. Brisbane sounded a little snippy, and I was GLAD-GLAD-GLAD. "Come on, Humphrey."

My classmates gathered at the door, waiting for my return.

"Back in your seats," Mrs. Brisbane told them. "And you, Humphrey, are going back in your cage."

I was so happy to be home, I took a long drink of water, then headed straight for my sleeping hut and a nice long doze.

WHISTLE: A shiny device that, when someone blows in it, makes an ear-splitting sound that can seriously hurt the delicate ears of small creatures like hamsters. *Use whistles sparingly, if at all.* (Some humans can whistle without a device, but hamsters never can.)

Humphrey's Dictionary of Wonderful Words

4

Spring Fever

"Wait-for-the-Bell-Garth!" Mrs. Brisbane's words jolted me from my nap.

Garth always jumped out of his chair just before the bell rang for recess, lunch or the end of the day. When Mrs. Brisbane reminded him, he sat back down until the bell actually rang.

"Now you may go, class," Mrs. Brisbane said.

Once the room was empty, she shuffled the papers on her desk. Then the door opened and in came Principal Morales.

"Got a second, Sue?" he asked.

"Of course," Mrs. Brisbane greeted him. "What can I do for you?"

"Ruth Wright put in a complaint. It's about . . . "

Mrs. Brisbane finished his sentence. "Humphrey."

The principal smiled. "Yeah. Just try and keep him in the classroom."

"I intend to," said Mrs. Brisbane.

"Don't worry." Mr. Morales chuckled. "She also complained about the squeaky door in the cafeteria, some fingerprints on the trophy case and the fact that the clocks are running thirty seconds slow."

"Well, she teaches P.E. I guess rules are very important to her."

Mr. Morales strolled over to my cage. "So Humphrey had a little adventure today? Maybe he has spring fever," he said.

"I think the whole class does," Mrs. Brisbane answered. "It happens every year. The weather turns nice and the class gets silly."

The principal leaned in close to my cage. "Well, no more silliness from you, Humphrey. You stay put."

"I will try because that Mrs. Wright is MEAN-MEAN-MEAN!" I squeaked.

Mr. Morales chuckled. "Aw, don't let it bother you, Humphrey. Mrs. Wright likes to complain."

Then he turned back to Mrs. Brisbane. "Don't forget, deadline's coming up, Sue."

"Sorry. I forgot. I'll write myself a note."

Mr. Morales smiled. "Great."

The bell rang again, and the principal excused himself. In seconds, my classmates came racing back into the room, pink-cheeked, out of breath and smiling. At least most of them were smiling.

"Good game, Tabby," Seth told Tabitha. "We almost won."

"Yeah, we would have if it wasn't for you-know-who," she answered.

Then she glanced at Garth, who was right behind her. He definitely wasn't smiling.

"Take your seats, children," Mrs. Brisbane said. "Get out your social studies books and turn to page 112."

Sometimes being a classroom hamster is like being a detective. You hear little bits of conversation and try to figure out what's going on. Like, what was that about Mrs. Brisbane forgetting something Mr. Morales wanted? She never forgets anything! And why did Tabitha say "you-know-who" instead of Garth's name? And why wasn't Garth happy, like everybody else?

I was sorting out my thoughts when something even more puzzling happened.

Rather than reading his social studies book, Garth was writing something in big letters on a piece of paper, but I couldn't see what he wrote.

He kept the paper on his desk and read the book, but he stopped to look at the paper once in a while. Then he wrote another word next to it.

I climbed up my ladder to see if I could get a better look at it.

"Og?" I squeaked softly. "Can you see what Garth wrote on that paper?"

I heard some gentle splashing but no answer.

Mrs. Brisbane started writing questions on the board, and soon my friends were busily writing the answers. This went on until the lunch bell rang.

My classmates all got up and headed for the door. Garth pushed forward, clutching the paper in his hand.

He paused near A.J.'s desk and dropped the paper in front of his friend, then hurried toward the door. A.J. stared at the piece of paper, crumpled it into a ball and dropped it on the floor. (Uh-oh. Aldo wouldn't like that!)

When Mrs. Brisbane got ready to leave for lunch, she spotted the paper on the floor, picked it up and smoothed it out. She frowned when she read it, then put it on *her* desk and left the room.

"Something is unsqueakably wrong between Garth and A.J.," I told Og. "I've got to know what that paper says!"

It's a LONG-LONG-LONG way from the table where Og and I live to Mrs. Brisbane's desk and it's a perilous journey, but once I'm curious about something, I can't get it out of my furry hamster head.

"Keep a lookout, Oggy, okay?" I told my friend. "I'm going over there."

He answered with a reassuring "BOING!"

I pushed on the lock-that-doesn't-lock and the door swung open. I took a deep breath and, as I had done before, grabbed onto the leg of the table and slid down so fast, I could feel the breeze ruffling my fur.

I zigzagged across the room, happy to be outside the ball, since I didn't have to worry about bouncing off tables or chairs. I quickly reached Mrs. Brisbane's desk at the opposite side of the room. I can't tell you how tall it looks from a hamster's point of view.

Between the chair legs were two horizontal wooden

bars. I reached UP-UP-UP, grabbed the lowest bar and slowly pulled myself up.

"Are you watching the clock, Og?" I squeaked.

"BOING!" Og answered.

Grabbing the next bar, I used all my strength to pull myself up. I was getting tired, but knowing that lunch didn't last very long, I wrapped my legs around the chair leg and slowly inched my way up to the seat.

I sat there for a few seconds, trying to catch my breath. I was still a long way from the desktop and that piece of paper. Above my head, there was a desk drawer with a handle on it. I had to leap up to grab hold of it— ooh, cold and slippery—and then I reached up for the edge of the desk and pulled myself up again, finally flinging my whole body onto the surface of the desk.

I lay there on my stomach, muscles quivering from all that work. It's a good thing I work out every day on my wheel and my ladder. It helps strengthen my arms. Or my legs. Or whatever.

"BOING-BOING!" said Og, and I didn't need to look at the clock to know I needed to hurry things along. I sat up and saw the piece of paper laid out neatly before me. Of course, to my small eyes, the letters were huge, I had to squint and strain to finally make out what it said.

DIRTY RAT

That was it? I'd come all this way and put myself in great danger to read the words *Dirty Rat*? I had no idea what Garth was getting at, although I knew that being called a rat, which sometimes happens to me, is not supposed to be a compliment.

Og began splashing wildly. I glanced up at the clock and OH-OH-OH, I barely had time to get back!

I had to take the quickest (though not the safest) route back, so I slid down the side of the desk, landed on the floor with a large thump, raced across the room and grabbed onto the cord of the blinds, which I always use for swinging myself back up to the table.

"BOING-BOING-BOING-BOING!" Og sounded like the fire alarm, but all I could think about was getting back to my cage on time. I heard the bell ring as I skittered across the table and swung the cage door behind me.

Every muscle in my small body ached.

"BOING!" Og twanged.

"The paper . . . says . . . *Dirty Rat,*" I told him, panting from all my effort. "But don't . . . ask me why."

All that work and I still didn't know what was going on!

My classmates began to trickle in from lunch. As usual, Miranda was with her best friend, Sayeh, and other best friends were together: Heidi and Gail, Seth and Tabitha, A.J. and—whoa! It was very unusual to see A.J. without Garth.

A.J. slid into his seat first. When Garth sat down, A.J. leaned over. I strained my small furry ears to hear.

"What was that about? That 'dirty rat' thing?"

Garth glared at A.J. "Friends don't pick their best friends last. Rats do."

"You're my friend," A.J. protested. "You're just not very good at sports."

"Like I need you to remind me," muttered Garth.

Right then, Mrs. Brisbane started to talk about seeds sprouting, and there was no chance to learn more about the trouble between Garth and A.J.

～·～

"Wait-After-Class-Garth," Mrs. Brisbane said when the bell rang at the end of the day.

"Og, did you hear that?" I asked. "She didn't say Wait-for-the-Bell-Garth. She said Wait-After-Class-Garth."

Og splashed a bit, but I'm pretty sure he heard, too.

The room emptied out quickly, and soon Garth was alone with Mrs. Brisbane. Being kept after class is never a good thing, at least in my experience. And in my months in Room 26, a number of my friends had been kept after school.

Mrs. Brisbane went to her desk and picked up the crumpled paper. "Did you write this, Garth?"

Garth shrugged.

"It looks like your writing," the teacher continued.

"I was just fooling around," answered Garth.

"I found it under A.J.'s desk," Mrs. Brisbane explained. "I thought the two of you were friends."

"We're not friends." Garth wrinkled his nose. "Not anymore."

Mrs. Brisbane sat down and looked thoughtful. "Would you tell me what happened?"

"I've got to catch my bus," Garth answered, looking toward the door.

"Think about it and we'll talk tomorrow." Mrs. Brisbane folded up the piece of paper and dropped it in her purse. "I'll just hold on to this."

Garth raced out of the door without looking back. Mrs. Brisbane stayed sitting in the chair. She stared at the student tables, the bulletin board, the chalkboard. She looked at the room as if she'd never seen it before.

After a while, she picked up her books and her purse and came over to adjust the blinds. "I hope you two can get along for the rest of the night," she told Og and me.

"We'll TRY-TRY-TRY!" I assured her, and I meant it.

Og didn't say anything, but I don't think he was mad at me or anything like that.

Maybe he just had spring fever.

RAT: A perfectly nice rodent with a bad reputation. Some rats make nice pets. There are rats of all shapes and sizes, but when one human calls another human a rat, it's never meant as a compliment.

Humphrey's Dictionary of Wonderful Words

Surprise from Outer Space

I don't know if I had spring fever, but I did have aching muscles following my adventure that afternoon. Besides that, I had a funny feeling in my tummy after I read the note that said *Dirty Rat*.

I ate a good helping of Nutri-Nibbles, but my stomach still felt weird.

Later, Og and I were both in a somewhat dreamy state when the door opened, the lights came on and I heard a familiar squeaking sound.

"It's Aldo!" I rushed to the front of my cage to greet my friend. I was hoping he would be a little easier to understand than he had been the night before.

"BOING!" Og sounded quite alarmed, and I could see why.

There was Aldo's cart, piled high with his broom, his mop and pail, lots of spray bottles and cloths and trash bags to be filled.

And there was someone pushing the cart, just as Aldo did every night during the week.

But that person was NOT-NOT-NOT Aldo!

"Eek!" I squeaked.

The person with the cart was much shorter than Aldo. The person had no mustache and had longer hair, pulled back in a ponytail. The person had on a red sweatshirt and gray sweatpants and black high-tops.

That person was definitely a girl. Or a woman. A female, anyway. And there was something strange about the way she moved. She tugged at her ear, snapped her fingers and swung her arms in an odd rhythm. Still, she straightened the desks, swept the floor, then mopped it (which Aldo didn't do every night). She even dusted the shelf where Og and I live, but she didn't seem to notice we were there.

"How do you do?" I squeaked up as politely as possible. "Could you please tell me, WHAT DID YOU DO WITH ALDO?"

Og seemed quite upset as he hopped up and down, up and down, repeating one "BOING" after another.

The person who was cleaning didn't even seem to notice. As she swept closer to my cage, I saw there was a device attached to her ear!

"Og," I said nervously. "I saw a movie at Seth's house once about an alien from another planet, and that alien acted very strange. Kind of like this person."

Og stopped hopping and started listening.

"You don't think she could be one of *them*?" I asked. "Because in that movie, the space aliens captured a human and took him to their planet. I mean, you don't think that happened to Aldo, do you?"

Og stayed very quiet.

"In the movie, the space alien had wires in his head, too."

I was sorry I'd seen that movie because it made me think scary thoughts.

"See that thing in her ear? She could be getting signals from the mother ship." I tried not to become hysterical. "That's what they called it in the movie. The mother ship."

Finally, the person, who had done a very nice cleaning job for a creature from outer space, wheeled the cart out the door. She turned off the lights (without opening the blinds, the way Aldo always did) and left Room 26.

The room was quiet, except for the TICK-TICK-TICK of the clock, which seemed to be louder than usual.

Suddenly, the lights came back on. The person walked back in without the cleaning cart. She came over to my cage and reached in her pocket.

"A ray gun, Og! The space aliens in the movie had ray guns so they could capture the Earthlings!" I squeaked.

She pulled out a small carrot and shoved it between the bars of my cage. Then she left again, turning out the lights so we were plunged in darkness.

"Eek!" I squeaked. When my eyes adjusted to the dark, I stared at the little carrot. "I guess that's not really a ray gun," I said. "But it could be an alien carrot."

"BOING!" Og agreed.

It was nice of the creature to give me a carrot, but I

have to admit, I didn't touch it. Not all night long. You can't be too sure about aliens, you know.

And I still had no idea what had happened to my good friend Aldo.

~•~•~

The world looked normal again in the light of day, and the morning went along like any morning in Room 26, except for the fact that Garth and A.J. were both very quiet. In fact, they never even looked at each other.

Then came time for recess.

While Mrs. Brisbane wrote word problems on the board, I spun on my wheel, knowing my friends were out exercising on the playground.

Suddenly, the door swung open and in walked Mrs. Wright, pulling Garth along with her. He looked very unhappy.

"Mrs. Brisbane, you'll have to do something about this boy!" the P.E. teacher announced.

Mrs. Brisbane was truly surprised. "Garth? What happened?"

"You know our students are required to get a certain amount of physical activity at recess every day," said Mrs. Wright. "But I found this young man hiding behind the building when he was supposed to be playing ball. *Strictly* against the rules."

"Were you hiding, Garth?" Mrs. Brisbane asked.

"Sort of," he mumbled.

Mrs. Brisbane told Mrs. Wright that she'd take care of the situation.

"What will you do?" the P.E. teacher asked, fingering her whistle.

"That's between Garth and me." There was ice in Mrs. Brisbane's voice. "Thank you, Mrs. Wright."

Mrs. Wright left, thank goodness, and Mrs. Brisbane asked Garth to sit down. She sat down next to him.

"Why weren't you playing ball with your friends?" she asked.

"Don't have any," said Garth. His face was squinched up like he was going to cry.

"Of course you do, Garth," Mrs. Brisbane insisted. "You have lots of friends."

Garth shook his head. "Not anymore."

Mrs. Brisbane spoke very softly. "Please tell me what happened."

"I'm lousy at softball, and when they choose up teams, I always get picked last." Garth's voice quavered. "Yesterday, A.J. was the team captain and got to pick his players and he picked me last, even though I'm his best friend. I mean, I *was* his best friend. He even picked Sayeh before me, and she's not very good either. Then Tabitha told Seth they lost because of me. So I decided not to play anymore."

He sniffled, and Mrs. Brisbane handed him a tissue.

"I'm sure that hurt a lot. It always hurt me when I got picked last. I wasn't very good at sports," she confided.

"But you're a *girl,*" Garth told her. "Girls don't have to be good."

Mrs. Brisbane smiled a little. "I understand that Tabitha is the best player in the class, and she's a girl."

"Yeah, but still, it's different being a boy." Garth sighed. "A.J. would probably pick Humphrey ahead of me."

Well, yes, he might. I'm very popular with my friends. I don't know how to play softball, but I have to admit, I am good at hamster ball.

Garth and Mrs. Brisbane sat in silence for a while until I just couldn't stand it any longer.

"I think A.J. was MEAN-MEAN-MEAN not to pick Garth," I blurted out.

"It sounds like Humphrey has something to say on the subject," said the teacher.

Garth didn't even smile.

"Tell you what," she continued. "You and A.J. bring your lunches in here today and we'll talk."

"He'll think I told on him!" Garth protested.

"I'll make sure he doesn't," Mrs. Brisbane assured him. "But I can't make him choose you first."

"Even if he'd picked me third or fourth it would have been okay," said Garth. "Just not *last*."

Mrs. Brisbane glanced at the clock and said that recess was almost over. She asked him to feed Og some of his yucky crickets, something Garth likes to do.

I headed for my sleeping hut to think about what I'd just heard. I didn't know a thing about softball. I'd never been chosen for a team, either. But I knew one thing: I wouldn't want to be picked last, especially by my best friend.

◡◠◡

Lunchtime rolled around, and Mrs. Brisbane told Garth and A.J. to bring their lunches to the classroom. This was a surprising thing that had never happened before, like being in a hamster ball or having Aldo captured by aliens.

A.J. brought his lunch from home in a bright blue bag. Garth carried his in on a tray, and it smelled yummy. Mrs. Brisbane took a container of yogurt and a spoon out of her bag.

But no one, not even Mrs. Brisbane, ate a bite.

"A.J., Mrs. Wright said that you picked a very good softball team yesterday," she began.

"Yes, ma'am," said A.J. loudly.

"But she was surprised that you didn't pick Garth until last."

A.J. stared down at the untouched sandwich in front of him.

"I was surprised, too," the teacher continued. "Since you're such good friends."

"Yes, ma'am," said A.J. "It's just, Garth's not the best player. And I think when you're choosing a team, you've got to pick the best players. Don't you?"

"I suppose so," said Mrs. Brisbane. "How do you feel about that, Garth?"

Garth squirmed in his chair. "It wouldn't have hurt him to pick me. I ended up on the team anyway."

42

"So it made you feel bad to be picked last?" Mrs. Brisbane asked.

"Yes." Garth looked miserable. So did A.J.

"Somebody's got to be picked last," said A.J. "The rest of the team would have been mad if I picked you before somebody like Richie or Kirk."

"I never thought of that," said Mrs. Brisbane, stirring the yogurt with her spoon.

"Well, now *I'm* mad, because it feels really awful to be picked last," said Garth. His cheeks were flaming red.

"I guess it does," Mrs. Brisbane agreed.

As far as I could see, the conversation was going nowhere. Back and forth, back and forth. Mrs. Brisbane agreed with both of them, but neither boy changed his mind. Not one bit.

"I imagine A.J. is sorry you felt bad," said Mrs. Brisbane. "Right?"

"Well . . . sure." A.J. didn't sound totally convinced, but at least he agreed.

"And I'll bet Garth realizes what a hard decision it was for you, A.J.," she added. "Right, Garth?"

"Yeah . . ."

Garth sounded like he had more to say, but Mrs. Brisbane didn't let him. "Good. Then you two can play ball together and be friends as well. After all, softball is only a game. It shouldn't be important enough to break up a friendship. Agreed?"

The boys nodded. They didn't have much choice.

Mrs. Brisbane wasn't quite finished. "Then at the next recess, you'll play ball, won't you, Garth?"

Garth groaned. "I'll just strike out and then everybody will be mad at me."

"You don't keep your eye on the ball," A.J. blurted out.

"I do, too," Garth snapped back. "I keep my eye on it as it sails past my bat."

Mrs. Brisbane glanced at the clock. "Eat your lunches now. You've got to keep your strength up for the next game."

She sounded very cheery, but Garth and A.J. looked about as un-cheery as two people could be. They ate their lunches in silence until I couldn't stand it anymore.

"For goodness' sake, make up!" I squeaked.

Mrs. Brisbane craned her neck to look at me. "I didn't know you were so interested in sports, Humphrey," she said. The boys finally smiled a little.

I don't know much about sports, but I do know about Garth and A.J. And if Mrs. Brisbane couldn't get them to be friends again, I guess I'd have to.

It's just that I didn't have a single idea of how I'd do it.

ALIEN: Somebody—or something—from another land or even another planet. Aliens can be any shape, size, color . . . but they usually want to take you to their leader.

Humphrey's Dictionary of Wonderful Words

The Space Alien Squeaks

Later that afternoon, when it was time for recess again, Mrs. Brisbane asked Garth to stay inside.

He looked pretty miserable, I guess because he thought he was in trouble again. But once the other students had left, Mrs. Brisbane told Garth he could read or erase the chalkboard for her or work on his homework.

"You're not in trouble, Garth," she explained. "I thought you'd like a break from recess, just for today."

He clearly did, because that was the cleanest chalkboard I've ever seen.

Once school was out, I didn't have much time to worry about Garth and A.J. I had creatures from outer space on my mind.

"Og, I've been thinking about that alien movie I saw at Seth's house," I told my neighbor. "They talked a funny language. Like they said *roka mata* instead of *hello*. And *oobo trill* instead of *good-bye*. They could understand each other, but no humans could understand them."

"BOING!" Og sounded truly alarmed.

"I was thinking, that night Aldo talked so strangely, maybe he'd already been taken over by space aliens."

"BOING-BOING!" Og replied.

"But the alien—or whoever she was—didn't say a word last night. Maybe she will, if she comes back tonight."

I was feeling shivery and quivery just thinking that a creature from another planet might return to Room 26.

The clock loudly ticked off the minutes as the room grew darker.

"It won't be long now, Oggy," I squeaked.

Og splashed around in the water. How I wish he could really talk so I could understand him!

Then I heard it: the SQUEAK-SQUEAK-SQUEAKING of the cleaning cart. My heart skipped a beat. Maybe Aldo would be back! I'd be so happy to see him, I wouldn't care what came out of his mouth.

The lights came on and the cart rolled into the room. It took my eyes a few seconds to get used to the bright light. When they did, I saw who was pushing the cart. It was the creature from the night before, only this time she had a hood over her head. I couldn't see if the device was attached to her ear or not.

As she went about her work, I wondered why space aliens would come to Earth to clean Room 26. And I wondered what this creature had done to Aldo. What was her evil plan? Just thinking about my missing friend made me angry. Suddenly, I wasn't scared anymore.

"PLEASE-PLEASE-PLEASE tell us what you did with Aldo!" I demanded.

Either the aliens on the mother ship told her to ignore me or she didn't hear me. She just kept on sweeping.

Suddenly, there was a loud noise—not exactly music, but not exactly a ringing either. It sounded like the music of another planet.

The mother ship was calling!

The alien cleaner tapped her ear. The music stopped.

"Hi. Yeah, it's me. I'm cleaning."

WHAT-WHAT-WHAT was going on? First she makes Aldo say things I don't understand and now *she* speaks English.

"I'm finished with the program. Yeah, I don't take off for Spurling till summer." She hesitated, then laughed. "Don't worry. It'll be a while before I'm performing surgery on people. Listen, I'll call you later. Bye."

She touched her ear again. Then she pulled a tiny piece of cauliflower out of her pocket. She walked to my cage and dropped the cauliflower between the bars.

"Here," she said.

Without another word, she pushed the cart through the door, turned out the lights and was gone.

It took me a few seconds before I could squeak at all. "Og?" I said. "Did you see that? She can talk to the mother ship through her ear. And she's taking off for Spurling. Ever hear of that planet?"

"BOING!" he answered, but it wasn't much help.

Spurling had not been one of the planets on our bulletin board, but I remembered that Mrs. Brisbane had said there were other solar systems. Maybe this strange creature was from one that was FAR-FAR-FAR away.

But that wasn't what made me feel shivery and quivery. "Did you hear her say she'll be performing surgery on *people*?"

"BOING-BOING-BOING-BOING!" Og was clearly alarmed. So was I.

"Maybe that's why she captured Aldo," I said. My heart was pounding. "Some kind of experiment. Thank goodness she said it won't be for a while."

Og responded with a huge splash as he dove into his water.

I stared at the piece of cauliflower. It's usually one of my favorite crunchy vegetables, but just to be on the safe side, I hid it down in the corner of my bedding, along with the alien carrot.

I was relieved to see that they didn't glow in the dark.

It was unusually dark in the room that night, since the creature didn't open the blinds the way Aldo always did. Surprisingly, I dozed off. But I didn't have a very restful night because of my dream.

I'm sure most humans would be surprised to learn that I dream when I sleep. Humans seem surprised at everything I do. "Look, he's spinning that wheel," they'll say. Or, "Ooh, he's washing his face!" (That isn't even accurate as I don't exactly use soap and water.)

They'd be even more surprised at the things they *don't* see me doing, like escaping from my cage and helping my friends solve their problems. Or writing in my notebook, which is something most hamsters don't do.

But they'd be *flabbergasted* (now that's a word for my dictionary) by my dreams.

Especially the one I had that night.

There I was, standing next to a spaceship that looked a lot like Aldo's cleaning cart. It was parked in front of Longfellow School, and I was surrounded by creatures that looked exactly like green, glowing carrots!

"Take us to your leader," one of them commanded me.

I was very confused because I couldn't decide whether to take them to Mrs. Brisbane, who is certainly my leader in Room 26, or Principal Morales, who is the leader of all of Longfellow School.

The alien carrots moved in closer.

"Take us to your leader," they began to chant. "Leader, leader, leader!"

"*Oobo trill,*" I said, remembering that those words meant "good-bye" in the movie I'd seen.

Then I took off running across the parking lot with the alien carrots following close on my heels.

"Og, help me!" I called out. "Oggy!"

Suddenly, I saw my green, googly-eyed friend gliding toward me, riding the top of his tank (the top-that-pops) like a skateboard.

"SCREEE!" he shouted.

I hopped on the back of the speeding top and we

zipped across the parking lot, leaving the space beings far behind.

When I woke up, I sleepily squeaked, "Thanks, Og," before I dozed off again, and that time, I didn't dream at all.

⌒·⌒

The next day, I was busy worrying about how it feels to be picked last for a team and about space aliens whisking Aldo off to the mother ship (wherever that was).

Somehow, I had to let people know what had happened to Aldo. His wife, Maria, would be worried, as well as his nephew, Richie, who was a student in Room 26. I watched Richie carefully in class, but he seemed just the same as ever. Maybe he didn't know his uncle was missing yet. Still, on Thursday morning, I woke up with a Plan.

It's very important to have a Plan when you want to accomplish something important, like saving a friend from beings from outer space.

I got my idea while watching my fellow classmates finish up the bulletin board. Mrs. Brisbane brought out a big pile of shiny cutout letters. She used them to spell out S-P-R-I-N-G. There were a lot of extra letters left over, neatly stacked on the floor right under the bulletin board.

When Mrs. Brisbane and the students left for lunch, I made my move.

"Og, I have an idea, but I don't have time to explain it. Will you watch the clock for me?"

"BOING-BOING!" Og twanged.

If there was one thing that frog was good for, it was for keeping watch when I was out of my cage. More than once, he had warned me when I was running out of time.

I flung open the cage door (thank goodness for that lock-that-doesn't-lock), glided across the table and slid down the leg.

Once I was on the floor, I had a clear shot between the desks and wasted no time in getting to the letters.

But once I was up close, I realized that they were MUCH-MUCH-MUCH bigger than I had expected. Probably five times bigger than I am, maybe more.

Still, when I have a Plan, I don't let anything stand in my way.

"Watch the time, Oggy!" I called out.

Og assured me with a giant "BOING!"

I stared up at the tall stack of letters. This was going to be a test of strength . . . and a test of my spelling!

When I first had the idea, I'd thought of spelling out something like: HELP! ALDO HAS BEEN CAPTURED BY SPACE ALIENS!

But with such big letters and so little time, I quickly changed my plan of attack. First, I had to get the letters on the ground, so I backed up, then ran forward at top speed.

"Hee-yah!" I closed my eyes as I hit the stack of letters, sending them scattering in all directions.

"BOING!" warned Og.

I glanced up at the big clock. Og was right. I didn't have a lot of time left, so I quickly went to work. Let me tell you, it's not easy to read those tall letters when you're a small hamster and they're lying flat on the ground. I stood on my tippy toes so I could get a better look.

Luckily, there were several *A*'s to choose from. I picked a red one and pulled it out onto the floor. The *L* was a little more difficult. It was upside down, which means it looked like a *7*. I turned it around and dragged it to the spot next to the *A*. The *I* and *E* were easy.

"BOING-BOING!" Og twanged loudly.

Uh-oh. A glance at the clock told me time was passing a little faster than I expected. I turned back and searched for the next letter.

There were plenty of *Z*'s but no *N*'s in sight. I'm afraid it took me a while to realize that a *Z* turned on its side looks like an *N*. And vice versa.

A-L-I-E-N. Not quite right yet, I decided.

"BOING-BOING-BOING!" Og warned.

"Okay, Og. I'm almost finished!" I assured him.

One more letter to go. I didn't want a *B*. A-L-I-E-N-B would be confusing. I didn't want a *C* or a *V* or a *W*.

"BOING-BOING-BOING-BOING-BOING!"

I didn't dare look at the clock.

"Where are you?" I asked. Just then I saw it.

"Good old *S*," I said, pulling the letter into place.

A-L-I-E-N-S.

It wasn't a full explanation, but it was the best I could do.

"I'm coming back, Og!" I alerted my friend.

I raced across the floor, leaped up to grab the cord of the blinds and madly started it swinging.

"SCREEEEE!" That was Og's most serious warning. As soon as I was almost level with the table, I let go of the cord and slid across the table, landing with a thud right next to my cage.

The door to Room 26 opened and I heard the familiar sounds of my friends chatting away as they came into the classroom.

"Take your seats," Mrs. Brisbane told them.

I was at great risk of being discovered as I darted into my cage and pulled the door behind me. Luckily, no one was watching.

"Thanks, Oggy," I told my neighbor. All I heard was splashing.

"What on earth . . . ?" Mrs. Brisbane stared down at the letters on the floor. "Kirk, is this more of your work?"

"Huh?" It wasn't one of Kirk's funniest lines.

"Never mind," said Mrs. Brisbane. "But remember, April Fools' Day is over now."

"I didn't do it," Kirk protested.

"LOOK-LOOK-LOOK!" I squeaked. No one noticed. I glanced at Richie. If only he understood that his uncle was in danger. "Richie, look!"

Richie paid no attention. He was busy scribbling in his notebook.

Mrs. Brisbane gathered the letters, stacked them up again and put them on her desk.

All that work for nothing! I was out of breath, out of luck and for once, out of ideas. So I did the only thing a small hamster can do: I took a nap. After all, I'd need to be alert if aliens from outer space invaded Room 26.

At the end of the day, Mrs. Brisbane asked, "Now, who will be taking Humphrey home this weekend?"

"Me!" a voice called out.

It was Heidi Hopper, of course.

Mrs. Brisbane shook her head. "You didn't raise your hand, Heidi. I think maybe you need another week to work on that. Now, who else would like Humphrey?"

Several hands waved in the air. Through the months, I'd gone home at least once with all my fellow students and they all invited me back again.

"Garth, is it all right with your parents?" she asked.

"Yes, ma'am. They signed the paper." He pulled a crumpled piece of paper out of his pocket and held it up. Mrs. Brisbane walked to his desk and looked at it.

"All right, then. Humphrey is going to the Tugwells' house tomorrow," she announced.

I felt sorry for Heidi, who looked so disappointed.

Garth, on the other hand, looked happy for the first time all week.

DREAM: Like a surprise, a dream can be good or bad. Dreams are pictures you see in your head while you are asleep. Daydreams, unlike other dreams, happen when you're awake. They can be very nice, but teachers don't like them.

Humphrey's Dictionary of Wonderful Words

Surprise Attack

That night, after dark, the being from outer space returned to clean Room 26. As nervous as I was about Aldo's disappearance, I was glad that she'd said she couldn't operate on anyone for a while. She wasn't going to take off for the planet Spurling until summer, so I had a little time to save my friend.

Still, when she came up to my cage with a piece of broccoli, I just had to squeak up. "Release Aldo right away! And go back to where you came from."

"Gee, you're a feisty little thing," she said.

That was a first. She was talking to *me*. "You're so cute, I'd like to take you home with me."

"BOING!" That was Og's reaction.

My reaction was to quiver and shiver, just thinking of being taken to the far-off planet of Spurling, home of the alien carrots.

"BOING-BOING-BOING!" Og twanged.

The creature giggled and then pushed the cart out of the room and turned out the lights.

The room was dead silent for a few seconds. Maybe

longer. At last, I stopped twitching long enough to squeak. "Og, she wants to capture us!"

Og splashed briskly.

"We can't let her do it!"

He splashed a whole lot more.

I was relieved to be going home with Garth for the weekend. But my friend Og usually stayed in Room 26 for the weekend, since he could go longer without eating than I could. I wouldn't rest easily, knowing Og might be going to outer space while I was having a grand old time with Garth.

~•~

"Morning, Sue. Got something for me?" Mr. Morales was all smiles when he came in Room 26 on Friday morning. His tie had little kites with red tails trailing down.

"Oh, sorry. I forgot again," Mrs. Brisbane replied.

The principal's smile quickly faded. "Is there a problem, Sue?"

"No, I just forgot. I'll bring it Monday," Mrs. Brisbane declared.

Mr. Morales looked a little worried, and I didn't blame him. Mrs. Brisbane had NEVER-NEVER-NEVER forgotten anything before. Goodness, if she could forget something important that Mr. Morales wanted, she could forget something *else* important, like helping my friends and me learn our vocabulary words!

I was worried about my teacher, and there was more to worry about. Garth and A.J. still weren't acting like old friends. In fact, Garth went to great lengths to avoid

A.J., which wasn't easy, because their desks were very close.

At the end of the day, A.J. tapped Garth on the shoulder. "You taking Humphrey on the bus?" he asked.

"No, my mom's picking us up," Garth replied.

"Can I have a ride?" A.J. was at least trying to be friendly.

"Nope. We have to stop somewhere on the way home." Garth turned his back on A.J. and came over to my cage. I could tell his feelings were still hurt.

He gathered up my cage, food and even the new hamster ball. While he did, I had a last-minute message for Og.

"I wish you were going with me, Og! I hope you'll still be here when I get back!" I squeaked.

"BOING-BOING!" he twanged at the top of his voice.

I wondered if there were any frogs—or hamsters—on the planet Spurling, but I didn't want to find out in person.

"Farewell, froggy friend!" were my parting words.

I'd had several adventures on the bus with A.J. and Garth, but on that day, Garth's mother picked us up in a very tall car. Garth's brother, Andy, was in the backseat.

"Ham!" Andy shouted. I didn't mind. He was little and didn't know the difference between a hamster and a ham yet.

The ride home was smooth, nothing like the bumpy bus. Strangely enough, we didn't make a stop, like Garth told A.J. Instead, we went straight home.

Once I was settled on the family room table, I heard an odd twanging noise that reminded me a lot of Og. Could my friend have come along after all?

"BOING!" went the sound. Then "BLING-BLING." That didn't sound like Og at all.

Garth came into the room, carrying a large stringed instrument. He ran his fingers over the strings and out came the sounds. "BLING-BLANG-BLING!"

It sounded quite nice.

"How do you like my guitar?" Garth asked.

"It's unsqueakably wonderful!" I replied. I was just sorry all that came out was SQUEAK-SQUEAK-SQUEAK!

"I've been taking lessons," Garth told me. "Want to hear a song?"

"Of course."

He strummed those strings and played a great version of "Twinkle, Twinkle, Little Star." I only heard two mistakes, and they were small ones.

"Bravo!" I squeaked when he was finished.

"Did you like it?" asked Garth. "Here's one called 'Down in the Valley.'"

He played it from start to finish, without any mistakes at all that I could hear.

"Bravo!" I shouted again.

My classmates constantly surprise me with their talents. Tabitha and Seth know so much about sports, Sayeh sings beautifully and Art can draw. And ever since his birthday party where a magician performed, Richie's been doing magic tricks. I could never figure out how he did them.

Now Garth was playing the guitar. I only wish our other friends in Room 26 could hear him.

When his fingers got tired, Garth decided to clean out my cage. He was very surprised to find the hidden carrot and cauliflower. "Hey, Humphrey, are you on a diet?" he asked me.

"Be careful," I warned him. "They're from the planet Spurling. They may not be safe!"

Luckily, he threw them in the trash and examined my food bowl. It was empty, so he knew I'd been eating something.

"I guess you were just full," said Garth. "But I'd better watch what you eat this weekend."

I could guarantee him I'd eat just about anything, as long as it was from the planet Earth!

That night, I was more awake than usual. Yes, I'm nocturnal, so I normally feel a little peppier at night than during the day. But what kept me awake that night was the thought of Og. I could almost picture him boarding the spaceship and taking off for Spurling.

I hoped they understood frog language there.

⌇⌇

"It's a beautiful day! We should all go outside," Garth's mom announced the next morning.

She was right. The Tugwells' yard was a carpet of green grass with red and yellow flowers blooming around the sides. Two-lips, Garth's mother called them.

Garth put my cage on a table on the patio. Garth's dad pushed Andy on a swing in the back of the yard while Garth's mom dug around in the dirt, planting seeds.

"Come on, Humphrey, you need some exercise," Garth said as he gently took me out of my cage. "Let's try your hamster ball."

I would have preferred to run freely in the grass—just like my wild ancestors once did—but at least I had the chance to roll *on* it. The grass looked even brighter and greener from inside the yellow plastic.

"Watch him go," Garth said. His mom, dad and brother gathered around. The sound was a little muffled, but I could hear them laughing.

It was harder to make the ball move on the grass than it had been on the slick floors of Longfellow School. The ground wasn't even, and once in a while, I'd hit a bump and veer off in an unexpected direction. But I didn't mind because it was fun to explore the yard on my own.

Garth's mom went back to planting seeds, and his dad helped her.

"Want to roll!" Andy insisted, so Garth showed Andy how to do a somersault. Then Garth helped Andy get his legs over his head and roll across the lawn.

"Roll, Ham!" Andy called to me. "Roll!"

So I rolled some more until I hit a hill. It wasn't a big hill, but it was enough of a slope for my ball to pick up speed. Faster. And faster. And a little bit faster.

It was fun! It was exciting!

It was also SCARY-SCARY-SCARY! I stopped walking, but the ball kept rolling. I knew that cars slow down when humans step on the brakes. Unfortunately, hamster balls don't have brakes, so I tried to flatten myself on my tummy, pushing down hard with my paws, hoping that would help slow the ball down.

It didn't. The ball rolled and rolled and rolled some more until it finally came to a stop near some bushes at the back of the yard. Whew!

The ball may have stopped, but my head was still spinning. I was tired and a little thirsty, but at least I was safe inside the plastic.

It was nice in the shade. Dark, leafy and quiet. A little too quiet.

I could hear Garth and Andy laughing, but they sounded very far away. And they didn't sound like they were looking for me. I realized that if they didn't miss me, I'd never be able to roll the ball back UP the hill.

I sat there in the ball, catching my breath and hoping to come up with a Plan. I was distracted, however, when a long, dark shadow fell over me.

I looked up and was shocked to see two beady eyes, a number of huge teeth and horrible long whiskers hovering directly over my head!

It was—oh, no—a cat!

"Eek!" I squeaked.

The face moved in closer to the ball. A long, pink tongue poked out from the sharp white teeth.

I might have fainted, but I didn't dare risk it. I needed

to stay calm to deal with this crisis, but, "Eek!" I squealed again. I didn't mean to. It just slipped out.

A huge paw dropped down on top of the ball. BOOM!—I fell flat on my back. Funny how I'd worried all night about Og's safety and here *I* was the one in great danger! (Well, that wasn't so funny after all.)

The cat leaned in closer and opened his mouth wider to show off his pointed teeth, just in case I missed them the first time. He took his paw off the top of the ball. Whew! Maybe he was losing interest.

But no, the next thing he did was lie on the ground with the ball—and me—between his front paws. Then he began a charming little game. He batted the ball from one paw to another, which made me feel like I was in a game I saw at Kirk's house. Pinball, they call it. BOP-BOP-BOP, the ball spun from side to side, and I spun, too. One second I was upside down, then I was right-side up and I also slid from side to side. This might have been the cat's idea of a fun game but not mine, because I was pretty sure I wasn't going to be the winner.

While I was being tossed around, I started wondering how easy it would be for the cat to open the ball and get at me. My cage, after all, has a lock-that-doesn't-lock. What if this hamster ball had a catch-that-doesn't-catch? The catch was . . . I'd be caught!

"Sweetums? Where are you, Sweetums? Time for din-din!" I heard a voice call in the distance. The cat's head suddenly jerked to one side. So this must be the Sweetums who was being called. While he was distracted, I hurled myself against one side of the ball, which then rolled down under a bush.

"Sweetums, Mommy wants her baby girl to come home! Din-din!" the voice called out again.

Oops. Sweetums was a girl. A downright mean one, too.

Sweetums poked her head under the bush and batted at me with her paw. Luckily, the ball was wedged against a branch.

"SWEE-TUMS!" The voice was more insistent. "Yummy din-din!"

I guess Sweetums decided that din-din in the dish was more of a sure thing than a hamster in the bush, and she trotted away, leaping over the fence and into the next yard.

I was relieved, but I was also a little lonely. And a little thirsty, too.

I suddenly thought that after Sweetums finished her din-din, she might come back to the Tugwells' yard for dessert. Namely me!

Speaking of the Tugwells, where *were* they? They seemed as far away as the planet Spurling.

CAT: Like dogs, cats are extremely dangerous creatures with sharp teeth, gleaming eyes, pointed claws and an appetite for smaller, cuter animals such as hamsters. If a cat gets hold of a hamster, it can lead to a *cat*astrophe, which I don't even want to think about.

Humphrey's Dictionary of Wonderful Words

The Hunt Continues

The Tugwells were looking for me. They just weren't looking hard enough.

I could hear them in the distance, calling my name and arguing among themselves.

"How could you take your eye off him?"

"I've looked everywhere!"

"Have you checked those bushes?"

"Of course!"

"We have to find him before dark!"

"Maybe we need some help."

"Help find Ham!"

I tried to move my ball, but it wouldn't budge. I was stuck.

It was quiet for a while, which made me a little nervous, but I tried to stay very still and rest. I tried not to think about water . . . or Sweetums.

I woke up when I heard big footsteps clomping through the grass.

Voices called out, "Humphrey! Hum-phrey!"

And one voice was so loud it was unmistakable, saying, "Humphrey, tell us where you are!"

It had to be A.J.

"I'm HERE-HERE-HERE!" I squeaked as loudly as a hamster can.

I guess no one heard me because the voices kept calling.

"Humphrey! Humphrey! Humphrey!"

"HERE-HERE-HERE!"

For some reason, we weren't making any progress.

It was quiet again, and then I heard more footsteps, thudding through the grass.

"Look over there," a small voice whispered.

"I'm here!" I squeaked.

"How about those bushes?" a second voice asked.

"OVER HERE!" I yelled.

Then I heard it. "MEEOW!"

I made the mistake of looking up.

Sweetums was poised on top of the fence, staring down at me. Din-din was over. It was time for dessert.

"UNDER THE BUSH!" I yelled at the top of my tiny lungs.

I heard more footsteps coming closer.

"Down there," said a voice. "Ham?"

That, I knew, was Andy.

"I'll crawl under there," said the other voice.

It seemed like a long time before I saw someone looking right at me. It wasn't Sweetums this time, thank goodness. It was DeeLee, A.J.'s little sister.

"Here's a ball. Aw, it's Humphrey. Come here,

honey." DeeLee reached in and grabbed the ball. She was a little rough, but I didn't mind.

"Hi, Humphrey." She had a big smile on her face. So did I.

"Hi, Ham," said Andy. I didn't mind being called a ham. I just didn't want to be called "dessert."

"Meow!" called Sweetums, obviously jealous of the attention I was getting.

"Hi, pretty kitty," DeeLee answered.

I cringed at her cat-friendly tone, but I forgave the girl, because she'd saved me.

Carrying the ball (and me), DeeLee raced up into the yard. "We found him! We found him!" she squealed.

Soon, all of Garth's family and all of A.J.'s family gathered around.

"Way to go!" said A.J., hugging his sister.

"Let's get him to his cage," said Garth's mom. "He needs food and water."

Boy, she sure got *that* right.

As we all hurried toward the house, I thought about Sweetums and how disappointed she must have been.

Too bad, I thought. I only hoped that Og was as lucky as I was when the aliens came to take him away.

❧

I drank and drank and drank. I know my friends drink juice and soda, but nothing in the whole wide world tastes better than water. Trust me on that.

Mrs. Tugwell served the Thomases lemonade and

cookies, and they all laughed and shared stories about me, Garth and A.J.

"When you called and asked if A.J. could help look for Humphrey, I said, 'We're all going,'" Mr. Thomas said. "We had to help out our little buddy."

"*I* found him!" DeeLee bragged.

And I was GLAD-GLAD-GLAD she had.

While the families talked, Garth and A.J. stayed unusually quiet.

"Why don't you take A.J. to your room?" Garth's mom asked.

"Okay." Garth didn't sound very enthusiastic. "Can we take Humphrey along?"

"Yes," said Garth's mom. "But be gentle with him. He's been through a lot today."

This was a very smart woman.

Once we were in Garth's room, the boys got quiet again.

"It wasn't my idea to call you," Garth finally said. "My dad made me."

"I'm glad he did. My sister found Humphrey, didn't she?" A.J. replied.

"Along with my brother," Garth snapped back.

They were quiet again. Under ordinary circumstances, I would have spun on my wheel to entertain them, but I was far too weak.

"What's that?" A.J. asked after a while.

"My guitar," answered Garth.

"Can you play it?"

"Sure." Garth took the guitar out of its case, fooled around with the strings, then began to play "Down in the Valley."

"You really can play," said A.J.

"I told you I could." Garth's voice had an edge to it. He started playing another song.

"I wish I could play." A.J. sounded wistful. "Can I try it?"

Garth thrust the guitar at A.J. "Okay."

A.J. tried to play, but it sounded AWFUL-AWFUL-AWFUL! We hamsters have sensitive ears, and mine were hurting from the terrible sounds that came out of the guitar.

He stopped abruptly, thank goodness, and handed the guitar back to Garth.

"Here," he said. "I'm no good."

"Nobody's good in the beginning," said Garth. "I've been practicing for months." He started strumming again, and it sounded good.

"Honey, we're going home." A.J.'s mom poked her head in the door. "Garth's parents said you can stay if you'd like."

"Okay," said A.J.

"Okay with you, Garth?" asked Mrs. Thomas.

"Sure," Garth answered, but he didn't sound as if he meant it.

After A.J.'s mom left, Garth and A.J. were quiet for a while, which wasn't normal for them. They stared at my cage, and finally Garth said, "Maybe Humphrey's ready for another spin."

My stomach did a somersault at the thought of meeting up with Sweetums again, but this time, Garth put me in the ball and let me roll around his bedroom floor. I was pretty tired of rolling, but I was also worried about coming face-to-face with another cat or a dog or some other dangerous creature. It was time for me to take charge of my hamster ball!

Garth strummed the guitar, but I hardly noticed. I already knew how to make wide turns, but now I wanted to try sharp turns. I spun my body to the right as fast as my legs would go, but the ball wobbled rather than moving very far.

A.J. laughed. "Look at Humphrey Dumpty."

Garth laughed, too. "He looks a little seasick."

Once the ball stopped wobbling, I decided to try again. I remembered seeing some boys on skateboards one time. They could leap up in the air and land, reversing the direction of their boards. I took a deep breath and leaped up, turning my body at the same time. The only thing that happened was I hit my head on the ball and did a double somersault, which is a pretty good trick, but not what I was aiming for.

Meanwhile, I heard A.J. ask Garth if he could teach him to play the guitar.

"I'll try," said Garth. He didn't sound too convinced. As the boys sat side by side on the bed, Garth showed A.J. where to put his fingers and how to strum the strings.

It still sounded terrible, horrible and VERY-VERY-VERY bad!

"I'm hopeless," said A.J.

"You could be good." Garth sounded a little friendlier. "Try it again."

I was already trying again. This time I didn't hit my head, and I kept my balance as I leaped to the right. And what do you know? The ball made a faster turn to the right. It was still circular, but I felt more in control.

A.J.'s guitar playing was way *out* of control.

"I give up." A.J. handed the guitar back to Garth.

Garth picked out a few notes. "It sounded terrible when I tried in the beginning, too. You just need practice."

Suddenly, A.J. jumped up and pointed right at me. "Hey, look at Humphrey! That's so cool!"

What I was doing was pretty cool, if I do say so myself. First, I made a tight left-hand circle. Then I leaped to the right and did a tight right-hand circle.

Garth and A.J. got down on their knees and watched me. "That's amazing!" A.J. exclaimed. "How'd he figure that out?"

"I think he was practicing," Garth said. "Now he could be in the hamster ball Olympics!"

"You know what? You could throw the ball better if you practiced," said A.J. "Don't you ever play catch with your dad?"

"Dad said he's not very good at playing ball," Garth told him.

"Oh," said A.J. Then after a while he added, "Maybe I could practice with you. You could help me with the guitar and I could help you with softball."

"You really think I could get better?" Garth asked.

"Sure," said A.J. "Look at how good Humphrey is at ball!"

And I was very good, indeed. Sweetums would have a hard time keeping up with me now.

Garth's dad popped his head in the doorway. "We're ordering pizza for dinner. You like pepperoni?" he asked A.J.

"Sure!"

"If you want to spend the night, your mom said she'd drop your clothes off," Mr. Tugwell added.

"Okay with you, Garth?" A.J. asked.

"Okay!"

I was glad to hear that Garth answered without a bit of hesitation.

Garth took me out of the hamster ball and put me back in my cage. While the family ate pizza, I took a long nap, and I dreamed about beautiful guitar music instead of space aliens or cats.

The next afternoon, A.J. talked Garth into coming outside. "We'll just toss the ball around," he said.

"I won't be good," Garth warned him.

"Maybe not, but you'll get better than you are now," A.J. said. "Just like the guitar. Or the hamster ball."

I was happy they left me in the house. Although I had a new technique, I wasn't anxious to come nose to nose with Sweetums again. She might still be looking for dessert.

Even though I was inside, I could still hear Garth and A.J. laughing and shouting in the yard.

"Nice catch," A.J. said once. "Way to go!"

I spun on my wheel with pure joy. Even without a Plan, I'd managed to help my friends. *That* was the best trick I'd learned all day.

PRACTICE: Doing the same thing over and over in order to get better at it (and all I can say is, if you play the guitar the way A.J. does, you'd better practice a lot). Practice always pays off, especially when steering a hamster ball.

Humphrey's Dictionary of Wonderful Words

No Surprises

"Well, well, if it isn't Humphrey." That's what Miss Victoria, the bus driver, said when she picked Garth and me up at the bus stop on Monday morning. "The best-behaved student on the bus!"

That was NICE-NICE-NICE to hear.

Things went so well between Garth and A.J. over the weekend that they sat next to each other and acted like best friends again.

As the bus approached Longfellow School, my whiskers began twitching and my fur began itching. Would Og still be there when I got back? Or had he been whisked away to the faraway planet of Spurling?

I'm happy to say, he was there! Nothing at all had changed in Room 26, thank goodness.

"Greetings, green and faithful friend," I greeted Og.

"BOING-BOING!" was his response.

Mrs. Brisbane walked over to the table by the window where Og and I live. "Are you guys glad to see each other?" she asked. "Humphrey, I was afraid Og would miss you over the weekend, so I took him home with me."

Whew! She saved him from an alien kidnapping and she didn't even know it.

"Lucky frog," I said. "The Brisbanes don't have a cat." I told him the whole story about Sweetums.

So there we were, back on the shelf by the window, and everything looked completely normal in Room 26. But the events of the past week made me realize how quickly things can change. Fire alarms can jingle jangle, best friends can become foes and things from outer space can invade.

During the morning recess, Principal Morales stuck his head in the door and said, "Did you bring it?"

"Oh, no! I forgot again," Mrs. Brisbane replied.

"Okay. I don't want to bug you. Maybe tomorrow?"

"I'll try," said Mrs. Brisbane, and the principal moved on.

After he left, Mrs. Brisbane said something very surprising. "It was only a little white lie." She said it softly to herself, but I heard it plainly. A little white lie.

I had no idea what she was talking about, but I'd never heard anything good about a lie. Even more confusing was the fact that Mrs. Brisbane would lie at all. She might be sad or even mad, but she was always honest.

I couldn't puzzle over what she said for long because my friends returned from recess. For the first time in a while, Garth came in with a big smile on his face. Tabitha slapped him on the back and said, "Good game!" Then A.J. high-fived Garth.

I guess all that practice over the weekend paid off, and I was GLAD-GLAD-GLAD.

But I didn't feel so happy later in the day. Mrs. Brisbane became extremely annoyed when Heidi Hopper blurted out answers—not once, not twice, but three times! (I was a little annoyed with her, too.) If Mrs. Brisbane had talked to her parents, it hadn't done any good.

After lunch, our teacher announced that we were going to have a surprise guest! That got my brain spinning as fast as my wheel. Could it be a magician like the surprise guest at Richie's party? Or maybe it would be Firefighter Jeff to help us practice Stop-Drop-Roll. (I hoped it would be him.) Just as I was getting excited, I realized that the guest could be somebody not so nice. It could be Mrs. Wright and her really loud whistle. Or it could even be a space alien!

I decided to wait in my sleeping hut. A small hamster can't be too careful.

It wasn't long before the mystery was solved, and no one was more surprised than Miranda—because the surprise guest turned out to be her father! I was almost as surprised as she was.

Mrs. Brisbane introduced him to the class and said, "Mr. Golden is an accountant. That means he works with numbers all day long. So he volunteered to spend the afternoon helping us with our math drills for the exams coming up."

Mrs. Brisbane is perfectly fine at teaching us all about

numbers and the things you can do with them, but it was interesting to see the way Mr. Golden taught. He and my friends played a cool quiz game that just happened to use all the math that would be on the test. Paul, who usually only comes into Room 26 for math in the morning, joined us for the fun. Even Pay-Attention-Art paid attention, and so did I.

I'd had a pretty exciting day, and by the time the last bell rang, I was looking forward to a quiet evening and nice, long doze.

Then I remembered the room cleaning. Would Aldo be back? Or would the space alien return? Would she be taking us with her?

I suddenly didn't feel like dozing, not one bit.

"Og? You know what to do?" I asked my friend later that night. It was dark outside, and someone would be coming to clean the room any minute.

He splashed around, which I decided meant "yes."

I'd used the time since school was out wisely and come up with a Plan.

I waited, I watched, I wiggled my whiskers.

And then I heard the squeaking of the cleaning cart.

"Remember," I told Og, "it's Aldo, we yell, 'Welcome back!' If it's you-know-who, we hide and stay perfectly still."

As usual, the lights were blinding when they were first switched on, but I made out the silhouette of someone too short to be Aldo. It was HER! I dove down and burrowed under the bedding in my cage, completely covering myself.

Things were quiet from Og's direction, so I figured he remembered his part of my scheme, which was to crouch down and hide behind a big rock.

If we both stayed perfectly still, the creature might not notice us and forget all about taking us back to the mother ship.

I could hear her moving chairs around, sweeping, probably dusting, emptying the two wastebaskets. I even heard her make that strange, otherworldly sound. Was that music—or vibrating signals from the mother ship?

"Yo," I heard her say. "Yeah, still cleaning."

Then she paused. "No. Just a few more days. Thursday's the big day for Aldo. Talk later."

I heard a click. There was more shuffling, then the lights went out and I heard the door close.

She was gone. That was good.

She was moving on soon. That was good, too.

But if Thursday was Aldo's big day, did that mean he was moving on with her? Because that was a VERY-VERY-VERY bad idea.

"DID YOU HEAR THAT?" I asked Og once the coast was clear.

"BOING!" I knew that was a "yes."

"Aldo's big day is Thursday. Does that mean she's taking him to Spurling with her that soon?"

Og couldn't answer that question and neither could

I. And I certainly couldn't sleep, not for the rest of the night.

⌒·⌒

My friends worked hard the rest of the week. In addition to Mr. Golden, Sayeh's dad and Tabitha's mom all came in to help the class with math.

While they multiplied and divided, I worried about Aldo and a different problem: Heidi Hopper.

There hadn't been any improvement in her behavior, but every day she asked Mrs. Brisbane if she could PLEASE-PLEASE-PLEASE bring me home for the weekend. And every day Mrs. Brisbane told her she needed to see some improvement in the hand-raising situation before I could come home with her.

I didn't want Heidi to be disappointed, so I worked on a Plan to help her remember to raise her hand. So far in my notebook I'd written

A PLAN TO HELP HEIDI
1.

I hadn't thought of one single thing, and I guess Mrs. Brisbane hadn't, either.

On Wednesday, tears welled up in Heidi's eyes when Mrs. Brisbane told her it wasn't looking so good for the weekend.

"I just need a sign that you're trying," the teacher said. "Couldn't you raise your hand just once?"

Heidi nodded, but she didn't seem sure she could do it.

Neither was I.

～∽～

Thinking about Heidi took up a lot of my time during the days, but in the evenings, I only had one thing on my mind: the alien. She said Aldo's big day was Thursday. By the time she arrived to clean on Wednesday night, I'd been spinning on my wheel for two hours straight, trying to whirl away my worries.

When she turned on the lights, I crawled under my bedding to hide. I'm quite sure Og slipped behind his rock.

I heard the usual sounds of sweeping and wastebasket emptying. Suddenly, there was that strange humming noise. The mother ship was calling!

"Hey, what's happening, Max?" the strange being said in a cheery voice. "Long time, no talk."

I took a big chance and poked my head out of the bedding.

"Oh, you'll never guess where I am." The space alien sat in Sayeh's chair and pulled her hood back. Her hair wasn't in a ponytail tonight. It was long and straight.

"Longfellow School! I'm not kidding," she said. "I'm cleaning."

She paused and laughed some more. "Seriously. I'm helping out my uncle Aldo."

Uncle Aldo? Aldo was an *alien's uncle*?

"He cleans here at night and goes to school during the day." She hesitated. "Yeah, he wants to be a teacher. But he ran into problems with Spanish. So he's got this huge exam and he's freaked out about it," she explained. "He got a tutor to help him study at night. Since I'm on break, I said I'd help him out."

"Og?" I asked in a shaky voice. "Are you getting all this?"

Og dove into the water side of his tank and splashed loudly.

The alien—I mean Aldo's niece—stopped talking. She adjusted the thing that was hanging on her ear. Maybe she wasn't talking to the mother ship at all. Maybe she was just talking on a phone attached to her ear. What a relief!

"I'm happy to help out Uncle Aldo. He's always been so great to me, taking me to the county fair and bowling, always ready to listen to my problems," she explained.

Yep, that sounded like Aldo, all right.

"He's the one who encouraged me to apply to med school at Spurling. Yeah. I start in June."

She stood up and started to pace around the room as she talked.

"It's really weird to be back at this school. It's the same as when I was here, only different." She examined the decorations on the bulletin board. "Everything seems smaller than I remember." Then she gasped. "Max, I can't believe it, but this is Mrs. Brisbane's class! *I* had Mrs. Brisbane! She was awesome! She was my favorite teacher."

She was staring at a big bunch of cutout flowers that Mandy had made. It was labeled, *To Mrs. Brisbane.*

"I can't believe I'm in Mrs. Brisbane's room," she repeated. "She made me believe I could do whatever I set my mind to—even being a doctor."

She listened for a while and then said, "Oh my gosh, I'd better get back to work! I'm only halfway done."

Still talking, she strolled over to my cage, reached in her pocket and pulled out something. I gasped, but then I saw it wasn't a ray gun. It was just a piece of broccoli. "I'm supposed to give the classroom hamster a treat from Uncle Aldo. There's a frog here, too. Uncle Aldo told me to talk to them, but I feel kind of silly doing that. I wish we'd had pets when I was in Mrs. Brisbane's class. Anyway, I've got to run. Talk to you later. Bye!" She tapped her ear and stopped talking.

Just when I was beginning to think Aldo's niece was smart, she said she'd feel silly talking to us!

But other than that, I kind of liked her. I wished I knew her name.

Og splashed away. After a while, I decided to eat the broccoli, because Aldo's niece wasn't from outer space after all. Spurling was a place on Earth, not some other planet. And the only reason she was going to perform surgery on humans was because—thank goodness—she was going to become a doctor! Best of all, I knew why

10

The Return of *Mi Amigo*

~·~·~·~·~·~·~·~·~·~·~

Heidi, do you know I really like you?" Mrs. Brisbane
had kept Heidi in during recess. I was expecting another lecture about raising her hand, and I think Heidi
was, too.

"Not really," said Heidi.

"Well, I do," the teacher told her. "You're smart,
you're funny and you're a very good student. I enjoy
having you in my class."

Heidi wrinkled her nose. "Really?"

"Really," Mrs. Brisbane replied. "I realize that I
haven't ever told you that. I've been too busy trying to
get you to raise your hand."

"Og, are you listening?" I called to my neighbor.

He splashed in the water gently. He was listening, all
right.

"That's a shame," the teacher continued. "I wish I
didn't have to spend so much time on that. But I worry that
your teacher next year might not get to know what a wonderful student you are, the way I do. I'd like you to break
that habit before you move on. Would you like that?"

Heidi nodded.

"I think I've made you very unhappy because you haven't been able to bring Humphrey home with you. Is that correct?"

Heidi nodded again.

Mrs. Brisbane smiled her kindest smile. "I think this weekend you should take him home. As long as you promise to keep on trying to break that habit."

Heidi's smile was as wide as her face. "Oh, thank you!" she exclaimed. "And I will try! I promise."

Mrs. Brisbane smiled, too. "Then it's all settled. Would you like to give Humphrey some fresh water and tidy up his cage?"

Of course she did.

"Oh, Humphrey, I can't wait till tomorrow so you can come home with me!" Heidi said.

I couldn't wait, either. But in the meantime, I had a lot to think about. It was Thursday, Aldo's big day, according to his niece.

Would he pass his Spanish exam? Would he come back to clean Room 26 again? There'd been so many surprises in recent days, I was looking forward to things getting back to normal.

It turned out I'd have to wait a lot longer for that to happen.

～⌒～

I was spinning on my wheel after school when Mr. Morales stopped by the classroom again.

"Just checking on that contract, Sue," he told Mrs. Brisbane.

Contract? Was *that* what he wanted from her? I stopped spinning and started listening.

Mrs. Brisbane sighed and shook her head. "I haven't been honest with you. I haven't forgotten the contract. But I haven't signed it yet, either."

Mr. Morales looked worried. "You *are* coming back next year, aren't you?"

Eek! The thought of Mrs. Brisbane not coming back to Room 26 was unsqueakable!

"I can't imagine not teaching next year. But this is my thirtieth year of teaching, and I qualify for full retirement."

Retirement? I panicked. When you retire, you don't go to work anymore.

"But you don't have to retire," the principal said.

"No. It's just, well, Bert."

Bert was Mrs. Brisbane's husband and a thoroughly nice human.

"He's had a rough year now that he's not working. I want to be there for him," she continued.

I guess he had a bad year, all right. He'd been in an accident and was in a wheelchair, but he could go FAST-FAST-FAST in it and he seemed pretty happy. He spent most of his time in his garage, making things out of wood.

Mr. Morales stood up and started pacing. In fact, he paced right up to the shelf where Og and I live. "I understand," he said softly. "I just can't imagine Longfellow School without you."

"Neither can I," Mrs. Brisbane agreed.

They were VERY-VERY-VERY quiet, and it was time for me to squeak my mind. "Neither can I!" I said. "And Bert Brisbane is doing just fine! Better than your students would do without you."

"BOING!" Og unexpectedly chimed in.

"Thanks for your support, Og," I told him.

Mr. Morales chuckled. "I think your friends Humphrey and Og want you to stay."

Even Mrs. Brisbane had to smile.

"Take your time, Sue," the principal said. "Just know what side I'm on."

I knew he was on the same side I was on. But would our side win?

Mr. Morales left, then Mrs. Brisbane left. Og and I had plenty of time to think over what we'd heard.

I looked out at Room 26, at the chalkboard full of math problems and the Spring into Numbers bulletin board, and tried to imagine Room 26 without Mrs. Brisbane. It was pretty hard to do. Of course, Principal Morales wouldn't let us students stay alone in the classroom. He'd have to bring in another teacher.

Suddenly, I *could* imagine Room 26 with another teacher, and it wasn't a pretty picture because the teacher I imagined was Mrs. Wright. It wilted my whiskers to think of her blowing her whistle at shy Sayeh to get her to speak up. Pay-Attention-Art would be scared silly if he happened to be daydreaming and Mrs. Wright blasted her whistle at him.

And my small, sensitive ears would be aching by the end of a whole day with Mrs. Wright in charge. Mrs. Brisbane knew how to handle my friends' problems without whistles or shouting or being mean. I started to imagine going home with Mrs. Wright on a weekend, but it was too terrible to consider.

Then I thought of another possibility. What if Mrs. Brisbane took me to her house forever? As much as I enjoy going to the Brisbanes' house, I couldn't stand the thought of not being a classroom hamster anymore. I wouldn't get to visit different homes or meet new families on the weekends. And who would help the students of Room 26 with their problems?

I poked my head out of the sleeping hut and loudly squeaked, "Og, you and I will have to stop her!"

Og took a long, loud, splashy dive into the water of his tank.

He had a lot of wonderful ways to agree with me.

•~•

I was still trying not to think about Mrs. Brisbane when I heard some wheels squeaking down the hall, toward Room 26.

By now, I was pretty sure that no spaceships were landing on the parking lot. But I wasn't at all sure just who would be pushing that cleaning cart.

The door swung open and the lights came on. Naturally, I couldn't see anything for a few seconds.

I held my breath and waited. I didn't have to wait long.

"*Buenas noches, señores,*" a voice boomed out. "You are looking at one very happy *amigo*. An *amigo* who has a bee-plus!"

The voice was definitely Aldo's. But I still couldn't understand everything he said. I knew he was happy. I knew *amigo* meant "friend." But why did he have a bee with him? Bees are annoying, noisy insects. And a huge bee-plus would be even more annoying.

My eyes got used to the light and oh—it was wonderful to see Aldo in his usual work clothes, his lovely mustache bobbing up and down above his smiling lips. He waved a paper in the air.

I got a B-plus on my Spanish exam!" He walked right up to my cage and waved the paper at me. "Okay, okay, I usually get A's on most of my tests. But this B-plus makes me very happy because I thought I might fail."

I couldn't imagine Aldo failing at anything. And now I understood that he was talking about a grade, not a buzzy insect.

"Congratulations, Aldo!" I shouted with unsqueakable happiness.

Og bounced up and down like the goofy frog he is. "BOING-BOING-BOING-BOING!" he twanged.

"*Gracias, amigos,*" Aldo answered. Then he looked around Room 26. "Say, the place looks pretty good. My niece, Amy, did a fine job. *¡Muy bueno!*"

"She did," I answered. "But I thought she was a space alien and I thought she captured you and I was SO-SO-SO worried!" I exclaimed.

Aldo laughed heartily, which made his mustache bounce. "I think you missed me, Humphrey. And you know what? I missed you, too."

Then Aldo, who has done some very funny things, such as balancing a broom on one finger, did something even funnier. He began to snap his fingers. Humming a peppy tune, he lifted his arms above his head and began dancing between the desks, tapping his feet wildly.

"Go, Aldo!" I shouted.

"¡Olé!" he shouted.

"¡Olé-Olé-Olé!" I chimed in.

I was so happy to have Aldo back, I forgot that Mrs. Brisbane might not come back at all.

At least for a minute, I forgot.

CONTRACT: A piece of paper that you sign as a promise that you'll do something, like teach school or pay your bills. Signing a contract is a very serious thing, and you should think carefully before you sign one. (Except for Mrs. Brisbane, who should sign that paper without thinking for one more second!)
Humphrey's Dictionary of Wonderful Words

Hoppin' with Heidi

~•~•~•~•~

Some things are not surprises at all. Like the fact that as soon as we got in the car after school on Friday, Heidi asked her mother if Gail could come over to spend the night. Heidi and Gail are BEST-BEST-BEST friends and do just about everything together (except once when they had a *bad* argument).

I wasn't surprised when Mrs. Hopper said "yes," either, because she's a very nice mom.

As soon as I was comfortably settled in Heidi's room, Gail arrived with her backpack. It wasn't long before the two girls were giggling.

"Let's dress up!" said Heidi.

"Okay," said Gail.

Heidi opened a big square box and the girls pulled out all kinds of hats and scarves and jewelry. "Let's be princesses."

Gail put on a firefighter's hat. It was just like Jeff Herman's hat, only this one was red. "Stop, drop, roll!" she shouted.

So I did. I dropped down in my bedding and rolled over three times. The girls didn't notice.

"No, Gail. Find something fancy," Heidi said. She had a shiny gold crown on her head.

Gail took off the firefighter's hat and poked around in the box. Soon the girls had on all kinds of lacy, frilly things and sparkly jewelry.

After a while, Heidi took off her crown. "Let's play a game."

"Okay," said Gail. "Let's play—"

"Cards!" Heidi interrupted.

Soon the girls were playing a game where they slapped down playing cards really fast. They were having such a good time, I decided to take a little nap.

I woke up when Heidi said, "I'm tired of this. Let's do something else."

"I have an idea," said Gail.

I never found out what Gail's idea was because Heidi said, "Time for smoothies," and raced out of the room. Gail sighed, but she followed her friend.

The girls returned a while later, with glasses full of something that was bright pink and looked delicious.

"Here, Humphrey. I brought you a treat," Heidi said. And what a treat it was: a big, juicy strawberry!

"I brought a treat, too," said Gail. She pushed a perfect little raspberry through the bars of my cage.

"THANKS-THANKS-THANKS!" I squeaked, which made both girls giggle.

"How about we draw pictures of Humphrey?" Gail suggested. I thought it was a very fine suggestion.

Heidi shook her head. "Not now. Let's watch the princess movie."

"Oh, I've seen that a million times," Gail said.

Heidi grabbed Gail's arm and pulled her toward the door. "So have I. It'll be fun!"

The girls were out of the room for quite a while, which gave me time to think. They were having a lot of fun, but I'd noticed something odd. No matter what Gail suggested—or tried to suggest—Heidi interrupted her with her own idea. And they always ended up doing whatever Heidi said. I was sure that Heidi didn't mean to be so bossy. In fact, I don't think she even knew she did it. But I was starting to wish that Gail could get her way for once.

That's when I came up with a Plan. I do like making Plans, so while I nibbled on the strawberry, I thought about what I could do to help Heidi see what she was doing.

I slipped my notebook out of its hiding place behind the mirror and turned to the page that said

A PLAN TO HELP HEIDI
1.

And I started to write.

~•~

Much later that night, my notebook was back in its hiding place and the girls were ready for bed. While they were in the bathroom, brushing their teeth, I opened the lock-that-doesn't-lock, quietly slipped out of my cage and hid under Heidi's desk.

The girls were giggling when they came back in. "I'll take the top," said Heidi.

"Okay," said Gail.

Heidi's bed was very unusual, because it was really two beds, with one stacked on top of the other.

Gail was already climbing into the bottom bed when Heidi said, "We'd better tell Humphrey good night."

Heidi leaned over my cage and said, "Good night, little Humphrey."

What she saw was an empty cage with an open door.

"Humphrey?" she said in a much louder voice. "Humphrey, where are you?"

From my vantage point under the desk, I could see the look of panic on her face as she twirled in a circle, searching every corner of the room with her eyes.

Gail leaped up. "He's not there?"

"No, look," said Heidi. "He's out of his cage."

Gail looked frightened, too. "I'm sure the door was closed."

"I know," Heidi agreed. "But he's not there! Oh, if anything happens to Humphrey, I'll never forgive myself!"

Gail looked around. "He has to be in this room."

Soon, the girls were crawling around the room on their hands and knees, calling my name. Finally, Gail spotted me. "There he is," she told Heidi in a loud whisper.

"Whew," said Heidi. "I'll get him." She crawled over to the desk and reached out to grab me, but I was way ahead of her. I skittered away to a spot I'd picked out under the bed.

Heidi looked pretty frustrated. "Humphrey! Why did you do that?"

I wanted to squeak up and say, "To help you," but I stayed quiet.

Gail closed the door to the room. "I have an idea."

Heidi jumped up. "I'll chase him out into the open and you catch him." She was already crawling to the bed.

"Come on out, Humphrey," she said.

She swung her arm under the bed. I came out, all right, and dashed under the dresser.

"Humphrey!" Heidi sounded irritated. "Come here!"

"He's not going to come to you," said Gail. "Listen . . ."

But Heidi didn't listen. "I'll get a cup and catch him in that. Keep an eye on him."

She raced out of the room. Gail sighed and stared at me. Heidi was back in a flash with a large plastic cup in her hand. "You chase him out into the open and I'll put the cup over him."

We played that game for quite a while. Gail chased me out from under the dresser. Heidi tried hard to put that cup over me, but I was too quick and too smart. Each time she thought she was going to be successful, I changed directions. I felt a little sorry for the girls. After all, it was time for bed. But I was determined to carry out my Plan.

Finally, Heidi stomped her foot. "This isn't working."

"No," said Gail. "But maybe . . . "

Heidi suddenly brightened up. "Wait—I know! We're doing it all wrong. We should move really slowly and tiptoe up to him so he doesn't even notice us and then we'll get him in the cup."

"I don't know." Gail sounded doubtful.

"Try it." Heidi was already tiptoeing. "We can't talk at all."

It was funny to watch the girls tiptoe around the room, trying so hard not to make a sound. To make it even more fun, I came out in the open so they'd think they could really catch me. Of course, the second Heidi started to lower the cup over me, I darted across the room and under the desk again.

"Bad Humphrey!" Heidi said. I actually felt like a bad little hamster, but I wasn't giving up on my Plan yet.

Heidi flopped down in a chair. "I give up. Don't *you* have any ideas?"

"Yes," said Gail. "I have a very good idea. Come with me."

Gail left the room and Heidi followed.

When they came back, without a word, Heidi moved my cage to the middle of the room. She opened the door and fiddled with it. Gail leaned down, opened her closed fist and placed something orange on the floor.

I stared out at the floor, trying to figure out what was happening. Then I saw it: a luscious, juicy, beautiful little carrot wiggling and waggling across the floor. I'd never seen a vegetable dance around like that before. I shuddered to think it might be an alien carrot until I noticed that the carrot was attached to a string!

This was my chance. I was longing to get back to the comfort and safety of my cage. Gail and her carrot gave me the perfect excuse to go back home.

I waited a few seconds before I ventured out from under the desk.

"There he is!" Heidi announced in a rather loud voice.

"Sssh!" Gail reminded her.

I stopped in my tracks, then headed straight for the carrot.

Gail pulled on the string, drawing the carrot closer to my open cage door.

She wiggled it and I skittered toward the carrot. She kept pulling the string and I dutifully followed.

At last, the carrot was at the cage door. She jerked the string and the carrot crossed over the threshold of the open cage door. I followed it and was back home again at last.

"Close it," Gail said, but Heidi was ahead of her. Bam! The door closed firmly behind me.

"We did it!" Heidi hopped up and down. Gail jumped up, too, and the girls hugged.

"I wish you'd thought of that a lot sooner," Heidi told Gail.

"I did," said Gail. "You just wouldn't listen to me."

Heidi stopped hopping and stared at Gail. "Yes, I would have."

"I tried about a million times," Gail explained. It was an exaggeration, but I understood how she felt.

"Heidi, you're my best friend and I have fun with you," Gail continued. "But every time I have an idea, you interrupt me and never give me a chance to talk."

Gail was following my Plan even better than I expected. It was all up to Heidi now.

"I do?" said Heidi.

"Sometimes," Gail answered. "A lot of times."

"I don't mean to," Heidi said. "These ideas just pop in my head and I say them. I'm sorry."

Gail gave Heidi another hug. "You're still my best friend."

"And you're mine," Heidi agreed.

Mrs. Hopper knocked on the door and said it was time for the girls to go to sleep. Soon, they were tucked into their beds and the lights were out.

"Tomorrow, let's practice being rock stars," Heidi said.

"I have an idea," said Gail.

I held my breath, waiting for Heidi's response. "What is it?" she asked.

"We could make up a hamster dance," Gail suggested.

Heidi was quiet for a few seconds. "That's a great idea," she said.

I was so happy that Heidi had listened, I did a little hamster dance of my own.

"Quiet, Humphrey," said Heidi.

And I was.

BEST FRIEND: A SPECIAL-SPECIAL-SPECIAL friend that you want to spend a lot of time with. A true best friend is someone who will tell you the truth (gently) and help you solve your problems. A true best friend isn't necessarily a human. A hamster can do the job very well.

Humphrey's Dictionary of Wonderful Words

12

Testing, Testing . . .

Any hopes I had that Heidi was cured of her problem vanished quickly once we returned to school on Monday morning. As soon as class started, she blurted out something about how great it was to have me at her house. Okay, she raised her hand in the middle of her sentence, but it was a little too late.

I had helped solve Heidi's problem with Gail, but that was only Step One.

Step Two would be to get Heidi to remember to raise her hand in class. And just like Garth, A.J. and me, she needed practice.

But I couldn't do anything to help Heidi for a while because Monday and Tuesday were testing days! For months, my classmates and I had been preparing for these big tests, and now, it was time. I wasn't sure what to expect, but I finally found out: these tests were very long, quiet periods where no one was supposed to squeak up at all.

No one did, except Heidi, who managed to say, "Mrs. Brisbane?" without raising her hand at least twice a day.

Unfortunately, I wasn't given a copy of the test, so I

spent those days catching up on my sleep. Or *trying* to catch up. Just as I would begin to doze off, troubling thoughts would creep into my mind and wake me up. Thoughts about how I missed Ms. Mac. I could still see her huge dark eyes, her bouncy curls and her great big smile. But over time, the picture of her was getting a little fuzzy, which was kind of sad. She was the first teacher who surprised me by going away, and I wasn't ready for that to happen again with Mrs. Brisbane.

I guess the contract was just a piece of paper, but I saw it as a SCARY-SCARY-SCARY thing. If Mrs. Brisbane didn't sign it, what would happen to me?

Then I thought about Mrs. Wright and her whistle. Whenever I pictured her, I would shudder and concentrate on coming up with a Plan to make Mrs. Brisbane stay.

The only good news during those days was when recess came and Garth and A.J. happily raced outside to play together. Garth didn't think A.J. was a dirty rat anymore and neither did I. Another thing that made me HAPPY-HAPPY-HAPPY was that Aldo was back to his old self: happy, laughing and full of life. I wished I could say "*gracias*" to the person who helped him study for that test! And I also wished I could ask him more about Amy. I tried, but even Aldo couldn't make out my squeaks.

I felt for my friends who worked so hard at their tests. It wasn't easy for Sit-Still-Seth to keep from wiggling or for Pay-Attention-Art to keep his eyes on the paper and not stare out the window. It wasn't easy for

Gail not to giggle, Kirk not to joke or Garth not to watch the clock.

Even super-students like Golden-Miranda and Speak-Up-Sayeh chewed on their pencils and sighed a lot while they stared at their papers.

"Why do we have to take these tests, anyway?" Don't-Complain-Mandy Payne grumbled during a break between tests.

"So you can prove what fabulous students you are," Mrs. Brisbane explained. "I know you'll make this school proud."

I knew it, too, but it was still hard to figure out how somebody could be graded on filling in little bubbles on paper.

Mrs. Brisbane, being a good teacher, made sure my friends took time to stand and stretch and relax between tests. Those moments made me feel good, until I remembered that she hadn't signed that contract yet and there was a very good chance she'd never teach again.

On Tuesday afternoon, just before the bell rang, Mrs. Brisbane made an announcement.

"The tests are all over, and tomorrow I have a big surprise for you!"

My friends cheered. So did I.

After class, Mrs. Brisbane gathered up her purse and her lunch bag. Before she left, she came over to check on Og and me.

"You know, Humphrey, I was hoping maybe you could cure Heidi of not raising her hand," she said. "But if I haven't been able to make a difference all year, how can I expect a little hamster to change her in one weekend?"

I had to squeak up. "I made a lot of progress," I told her. "We just have to get her to practice."

Mrs. Brisbane grinned mischievously. "Sounds like you have an idea! Well, so do I, and you can help! See you tomorrow."

She left quickly and I hopped on my wheel and spun with delight. Wednesday couldn't come fast enough for me!

My whiskers wiggled with excitement when the morning bell rang and Mrs. Brisbane began class.

"You all worked so hard on your tests, I'm very proud of you," she announced after the bell rang. "So today, we're going to have some fun!"

My friends cheered and I let out an extra-loud squeak. Even Og let out a joyous "BOING!"

"Let's just call this Wacky Day. Or how about Wacky Wednesday?"

Stop-Giggling-Gail led a chorus of laughter, and Mrs. Brisbane explained the rules for the day. First, she gave her desk to Og and me. That's right—she asked Richie and Seth to move Og and me from our spots by the window to the top of her desk. "I'll let them be in charge today."

I LIKED-LIKED-LIKED that idea.

Then she asked all the students to change seats. "Get as far away from your regular seat as possible," she said.

There was quite a commotion as my friends all raced around to switch seats.

Once they were settled, Mrs. Brisbane explained the rest of the rules:

- All students who were right-handed should use their left hands to write or draw. All students who were left-handed should use their right hands to write or draw.

- Students should blurt out questions and answers and should *not* raise their hands. If a student accidentally waved his or her hand, the other students were required to jump up, wiggle their arms and legs and make monkey sounds.

My fellow classmates loved that idea, especially when Mrs. Brisbane let them practice their monkey motions. I joined in.

"Look at Humphrey. He's a monkey, too!" Art shouted. (For once, he was paying attention.) My friends loved it, even Mrs. Brisbane.

So far, Wacky Wednesday was great, and it got wackier as the day wore on.

First, we had the Wrong-Hand Art Contest. Everybody had to use the hand they didn't usually draw with. I tried it and it was HARD-HARD-HARD.

"My baseball player looks like he's from outer space." Kirk chuckled.

He was joking, but I still didn't like to think about aliens.

To squeak the truth, the drawings all looked pretty strange. Tabitha won the contest because it turns out she can use both paws—I mean hands—equally well!

Then there was the trivia game. The class had to be divided into two teams. Guess who Mrs. Brisbane asked to be a captain? Garth Tugwell, the boy who hated getting picked last. The other team captain was Miranda Golden.

"You go first, Garth," Mrs. Brisbane told him.

Garth looked out at his fellow classmates. His eyes rested on A.J., and I was sure he was going to pick him first. Instead, he turned to Mrs. Brisbane and asked, "Wouldn't it be more fair just to count off?"

Mrs. Brisbane had a funny smile on her face as she nodded. "I think that would be very fair, Garth."

So the rest of the students called out alternating numbers one, two, one, two, one, two. All the ones lined up next to Garth. All the twos lined up next to Miranda. The funny thing was that A.J. ended up on Garth's team after all.

Next, Mrs. Brisbane asked funny questions, like, "Where did Dracula live?"

Garth had no trouble answering that one. "Transylvania."

As I recall, Dracula is a vampire with sharp teeth, so I hope I never have to go to Transylvania.

Mrs. Brisbane turned to Miranda and asked, "What does the legend say you'll find at the end of a rainbow?"

Miranda correctly answered, "A pot of gold."

And so the trivia game continued. A person who missed the answer had to sit down. The first one was Pay-Attention-Art. I guess he stopped paying attention again.

The next to miss was Mandy. "Can't I try again?" she begged.

Mrs. Brisbane told her to take her seat, but she said it kindly.

On the second round, Mrs. Brisbane asked A.J., "What weighs more: a ton of feathers or a ton of bricks?"

A.J. quickly answered, "Bricks." I think he knew it was wrong as soon as he said it, but it was too late. He had to take his seat while the teacher explained that a ton of feathers and a ton of bricks weigh exactly the same: they both weigh a ton, which is two thousand pounds. She is a very tricky questioner!

"Did you get that one, Og?" I squeaked.

The loud splash I heard made me think that perhaps he'd guessed the same thing A.J. did.

"Sorry," I heard A.J. tell Garth as he passed by him.

"No problem," Garth replied.

My friends in Room 26 are pretty smart, and it took

a long time before Sayeh and Garth were the only ones left standing.

Mrs. Brisbane asked Sayeh how many cookies are in a "baker's dozen."

Sayeh, who is hardly ever wrong, answered, "Twelve."

"Sorry, that's wrong," said Mrs. Brisbane. "Garth, do you know the answer?"

Garth took off his glasses and cleaned them with his shirt. Then he put his glasses back on and said, "Thirteen."

"That is correct," Mrs. Brisbane said. "If you answer the next question correctly, you win. What did Prince Charming have to do to wake up Sleeping Beauty?"

Garth grinned. "Kiss her!" he answered. Then, making a face, he added, "Yuck!"

So Garth and his team were the winners of the trivia game. As much as I love Miranda, this time I was happy Garth won. When Miranda high-fived him with a big smile on her face, I knew she was GLAD-GLAD-GLAD, too.

Late in the afternoon, Mrs. Brisbane played a brain teaser game with our class. She would ask a trick question. The first person to answer correctly received a cool sticker with a riddle on it.

The first question was: "Why can't a man living in the United States be buried in Canada?"

Sayeh raised her hand first. This was a good thing, because Sayeh is quiet and sometimes doesn't answer at all. But it was a bad thing, because according to the rules of the day, we weren't supposed to raise our hands.

"Class? Sayeh raised her hand," Mrs. Brisbane said. "What do we do?"

Kirk was the first one to jump up and my other friends followed. I joined in, too, as we made funny monkey sounds and jumped around. Even Mrs. Brisbane tried it. Nobody laughed harder than Sayeh.

Once everyone was seated again, Mrs. Brisbane repeated the question. Tabitha, Art, Kirk, Heidi and Sayeh all shouted out, but since A.J. has the loudest voice, he was the one I heard. "Because he's still alive!" his voice boomed out.

"That's correct," Mrs. Brisbane replied. "You can't bury a person who's still living."

The next question was just as tricky. "If you only had one match and you walked into a room where there was a candle, an oil lamp and a wood-burning stove, which one would you light first?"

Voices shouted out and I couldn't understand one of them. Heidi looked very frustrated as she waved her hand in the air. When they saw her, the other students leaped up and did the monkey imitation. Heidi seemed annoyed. "I *know* the answer, but no one can hear me."

"The candle!" shouted Mandy.

"No, the match," said Art.

The match was the correct answer, even though I would have voted for the stove. It turns out you can't light anything else in the room without lighting the match first!

The same thing happened with the next question

and the one after that. Heidi couldn't make herself heard. Finally, she stood up. "Mrs. Brisbane, I don't think it's fair because the winner is always the person who's the loudest!"

Mrs. Brisbane bit her lip and looked thoughtful. "Do you think it would be more fair if people raised their hands?"

Heidi nodded. "Yes, and you could call on the first person to raise her hand."

"So you agree that by raising our hands, this game would run in a fair and orderly way?" asked the teacher.

"Yes!" Heidi sounded very sure.

"Then maybe tomorrow when we go back to our regular rules, you can remember to raise your hand. Do you think you can, Heidi?"

Heidi's face turned bright pink. "Yes," she said. "I can."

Brilliant! Mrs. Brisbane had showed Heidi why it's important to raise your hand, she'd made it fun and everyone—including me—had helped. When class ended that day, I was convinced the she was the BEST-BEST-BEST teacher in the whole wide world.

I was also convinced that I'd be unsqueakably sad if she didn't come back to Room 26.

WACKY: Crazy, silly, goofy, loony, nutty, wild, and if a Wednesday is wacky, it's FUN-FUN-FUN!

Humphrey's Dictionary of Wonderful Words

13

The Big Break

"That was the Wackiest Wednesday ever, wasn't it?" I happily squeaked to Og when we were alone.

"BOING-BOING!" he twanged.

"And weren't you HAPPY-HAPPY-HAPPY to see Heidi raise her hand?" I asked him.

All I heard was a huge splash, but it sounded like a happy splash to me.

I was so excited about our funny day, I jumped on my wheel and spun as fast as I could. When I got tired of that, I spun the wheel the opposite direction for a while. I was tired and happy by the time Aldo came in to clean the room.

"*Hola, amigos,*" he said when he arrived.

I'd figured out some more Spanish by then and I knew that *hola* meant "hello."

"*Hola* right back at you," I squeaked.

Aldo was cheerier than ever since his Spanish test was over. He hummed and sang and waltzed his broom across the floor. The nightly show Aldo put on was better than anything I'd seen on television at my friends' houses. When he finished, he offered me bits of lettuce while he ate his sandwich.

"Well, *amigo*, it's time to say *adiós* and move on." He stood up to arrange his bucket, broom and rags on his cleaning cart. "I won't see you for a while. I hope you enjoy your trip, wherever you are going."

Aldo was saying strange things again! I was so stunned, he was halfway out the door before I could squeak, "But I'm not going anywhere!" It was too late for him to hear me. He was gone.

I didn't think I was going anywhere, but Aldo seemed pretty sure.

"The contract!" I told Og. "If Mrs. Brisbane doesn't sign the contract, I might be going away."

Og didn't respond. Maybe he was as worried as I was. After all, if I went away, he probably would, too.

As I lay in my sleeping hut that night, I thought about my future. Maybe I was going to live with the Brisbanes. Maybe I was going back to Pet-O-Rama. Maybe *real* space aliens were coming to take me away. None of those thoughts made me very happy.

At least Aldo had said "for a while." I hoped he meant that someday I'd be coming back to Room 26, the place I like best in the world.

The next two days, my friends seemed sillier and more excited than usual while I was much more serious. I think Mrs. Brisbane was, too, especially when Principal

Morales came in during recess to remind her about the contract. "Think it over next week, Sue," he told her. "I know you'll make the right decision."

On Friday, just before my classmates returned from recess, I looked up to see Mrs. Wright standing in the doorway. Her silver whistle glittered.

"Mrs. Brisbane, I just want to say that Garth Tugwell is participating much more now. And his skills are improving."

"I'm so glad," Mrs. Brisbane answered.

"However, two of your students came out to recess without jackets or sweaters on. It's exactly sixty-five degrees outside, and the rules say students must wear jackets or sweaters when the temperature is below seventy. I'm sure you'll remember that rule from now on."

"I don't think it's a very good rule," Mrs. Brisbane answered. "If the children play hard, they'll get overheated, which is just as bad as being cold."

Mrs. Wright did something funny with her eyebrows and they came down low over her eyes. I think that's called a scowl. "If you don't like the rules, then why don't you make a proposal to change them? That's why the principal has a suggestion box outside his office."

"That's a good idea," Mrs. Brisbane said. "I think I will!"

The bell rang and Mrs. Wright left, thank goodness.

"Ooh!" Mrs. Brisbane made a fist and pretended to pound her forehead with it. "Maybe I wouldn't miss this place so much after all!" she said. I think she was talking to herself, but I heard her say it.

"But we'd miss you!" I squeaked. "You have to stay!"

Mrs. Brisbane swung around to face my side of the room. "Humphrey, I hope you're not agreeing with that woman."

"NO-NO-NO!" I assured her.

~•~

All day long, I kept my eye on Heidi. Once she started to blurt out an answer, but I shouted, "Hands, please!" and even if she didn't understand my squeaking, she got the message and raised her hand.

When the day was almost over, Mrs. Brisbane asked my friends to clean up their tables and the area around them. "We'll be gone for a week for spring break," she said. "We want to come back to a nice room."

Spring break? Was something going to be broken? And where were we going for a whole week?

"Eek!" I squeaked.

Heidi's hand shot up. My, I was proud. When Mrs. Brisbane called on her, she asked, "Where will Humphrey and Og spend vacation?"

"Humphrey and Og will be at my house," the teacher answered. A few kids groaned, and she asked what was wrong.

"I wish I could have Humphrey for a whole week," said Garth.

"Me, too," Miranda agreed.

Knowing that Sweetums could get in Garth's back-yard and knowing that Miranda has a dangerous dog, Clem, living at her house made me VERY-VERY-VERY glad I was going home with Mrs. Brisbane.

I knew I'd be safe there and maybe—just maybe—a small hamster with a Plan could convince her to sign that contract and come back to Room 26.

All I needed was that Plan.

⌒⌒⌒

"Bert? Are you here?" Mrs. Brisbane opened the front door of the house. Bert didn't seem to be around.

"I'll bet he's in the garage," she said. She put my cage on the living room table. "I'd better bring Og in."

It was nice to be back at the Brisbanes' house. Next to my cage was a vase of pink and white flowers. Mrs. Brisbane always had flowers in her house—real ones. Soon, Og's tank was next to me on the table.

"Nice to be back, hey, Oggy?" I asked my companion.

"BOING!" he twanged.

I do like visiting the Brisbanes, I really do. But the thought of never seeing my friends in Room 26 was still a worry. *If* Mrs. Brisbane didn't sign that contract.

Mrs. Brisbane left again, and when she returned, her husband came in his wheelchair behind her. A smile now replaced the grumpy old frown he had the first time I saw him.

"My two favorite buddies!" he exclaimed when he saw us. "I've missed you."

"You spend so much time in the garage, you wouldn't know if they were here or not," Mrs. Brisbane said in a teasing way.

"I used to spend my time cooped up in an office. I love having that whole garage all to myself," he said. "I'll have to show you my latest creation: a three-story birdhouse."

Mr. Brisbane liked to make things. The best thing he'd made was my large cage extension with all kinds of wonderful places to hide, swing and climb.

"I guess you're happy to have a break," he said to Mrs. Brisbane.

"Yes, I am," she said. "Especially after today. Ruth Wright complained that I let some children go out without sweaters when it was sixty-five degrees instead of seventy. Is that all school has become: rules about sweaters and fire drills instead of teaching children to learn and grow?"

"It never will be with you around, honey," he answered.

"She said I should put my suggestions in the suggestion box. Well, I have a suggestion for her!" Mrs. Brisbane was getting pretty heated.

"I suggest you come out and see my birdhouse," he said. "And that afterward, we order some Chinese food and watch a movie."

Mrs. Brisbane gave his cheek a little pinch. "You're the smartest man I know," she said.

Maybe Bert could figure out a way to get her to sign the contract.

◦‿◦

The next morning, Mrs. Brisbane went shopping for new spring clothes. As soon as she left, Bert came to talk to me.

"Humphrey, I've got to go somewhere, and it just occurred to me that it would be a very good idea for you to come along."

Since I am a hamster in a cage, people hardly ever take me with them when they go out. I've never been to a restaurant, a movie or a mall. I've never been bowling, skating or camping. Wherever Mr. Brisbane was going, I wanted to be with him.

"Let's GO-GO-GO!" I said.

◦‿◦

I didn't know where we were GO-GO-GOING, but it was fun to be heading out with Mr. Brisbane. It took a while for him to get me, his wheelchair and himself in the car, but it was a beautiful day and I was excited to go somewhere new.

As he was driving, Mr. Brisbane said, "I didn't ask for permission to bring you along today, but I'm counting on you to win them over."

Win them over? When *didn't* I win humans over? I just didn't know which humans he meant. Because if one of them happened to be Mrs. Wright, I'd have to work pretty hard.

Suddenly, the car made a sharp right turn. "Welcome to Maycrest Manor," Mr. Brisbane said. "Today we're having a surprise party. And you, Humphrey, are the surprise!"

No one was more surprised than I was.

BREAK: Another good/bad thing. If you break your arm or a vase, it's a bad thing. But a break in school is like a vacation, and vacations are definitely good things.

Humphrey's Dictionary of Wonderful Words

A Day at Maycrest Manor

efore we went inside, Mr. Brisbane covered my cage with a cloth. "Just for a few minutes, buddy," he told me.

Still, I could peek out just enough to see that Maycrest Manor was a huge building with lots of tall windows, plants and trees. Inside, I saw people with canes and walkers and wheelchairs, and there were other people in colorful uniforms helping them out.

"Hi, Bert," a friendly voice called out. "What have you got there?"

He lifted a corner of the cloth and said, "Joyce, meet Humphrey. He's today's entertainment."

"Great! You can go right to the recreation room. We'll bring in the folks in about five minutes."

We took an elevator, which always makes my tummy feel queasy and uneasy, and then entered a great big room with chairs and tables all around. Mr. Brisbane wheeled us over to a table in the center.

"The people here are all trying to recover from illnesses and injuries so they can go back home again. I was here for a while last year, and they helped me a lot," Mr. Brisbane explained. "Now I want to help them back. All you have to do is be yourself, Humphrey." As if I could be anybody else!

Soon, the people in uniforms helped the people with canes and walkers and wheelchairs come in the room. I peeked out as they all gathered around the table. I was used to having giggly, wiggly children around me, but these were tired and serious faces.

"Okay, Bert. They're all here," the woman called Joyce said.

"Good morning," said Bert in a cheerier-than-usual voice. "I brought you a visitor today. His name is Humphrey. I know how hard you all work at your exercises every day, so I thought maybe you'd like to watch Humphrey work out." He pulled the cloth off my cage.

There was no reaction, just unsmiling faces staring at me from all sides of the table.

Bert had said *I* was the entertainment, so I decided to be entertaining. I jumped on my wheel, just to get things rolling. Then I leaped up onto my tree branch and began to climb. I didn't dare look at the faces around me, but I heard a little commotion. Next, I dropped down onto my bridge ladder and hung from one of the rungs.

Surprise, surprise, I heard chuckles.

"Look at that little fellow!" someone said.

Then I let go and slid down to the floor of my cage. I burrowed into my bedding and temporarily dropped out of sight.

"Where'd he go?" I heard a voice ask.

"Just watch," Bert said.

Keeping low to the ground, I tunneled through the bedding and suddenly popped up on the other side of my cage.

"SURPRISE-SURPRISE-SURPRISE!" I squeaked.

This time people laughed. When I looked at the faces again, many of them were smiling and all of them were leaning in to watch me more closely.

"Of course, Humphrey doesn't always stay in his cage," Mr. Brisbane said. He opened the cage door and put me in my yellow hamster ball. I hadn't even seen him bring it along. "Sometimes, he likes to go for a walk."

He gently set me and the ball on the floor. "Go for it, Humphrey."

I could see a lot of feet making way for me, so I started walking to propel the ball forward. Since I'd learned how to control my right and left turns, I decided to zigzag across the room. After a while, I looked back and saw that many of the patients were following me. Some of them were helped by the people in uniform. Some of them were on their own.

"He's over in the corner!" a man in a wheelchair announced.

Another man waved his cane at me. "Look out, here he comes again."

"If I had one of those contraptions, I could go anywhere," a woman with a walker said with a laugh.

It became a fun game of Follow the Leader, and I got to be the leader. It was a lovely afternoon, and we all got a good workout. Those serious faces looked a little less serious as my new friends told me good-bye.

When it was time to leave, Joyce was very pleased. "Bert, can you stop by my office on the way out?" she asked.

That's how I ended up on Joyce's desk while she talked to Mr. Brisbane.

"Boy, did that work well! Humphrey got them moving like nobody else," she said.

"He did the same for me," Mr. Brisbane said.

Then something amazing happened. Joyce offered Mr. Brisbane a job as recreation manager. He'd work for Joyce, who was too busy to come up with new and interesting projects for the patients. And they'd even pay him!

Bert accepted, saying he'd have to talk it over with his wife, but he was sure she'd be pleased. So was I.

⁓⁓

That evening, I was back on the living room table when Mr. Brisbane told Mrs. Brisbane the good news. "I'd sure like to go to work every day," he said. "And I'd enjoy that work more than I ever liked my old job. What do you think, Sue?"

Mrs. Brisbane looked surprised—no, stunned. Then she burst out laughing.

"What's so funny?" Mr. Brisbane asked.

"Oh, Bert, I've been trying to figure out how to talk to you about this. I still haven't signed my contract for next year."

Mr. Brisbane looked surprised. "Why not?"

"This is my thirtieth year," his wife replied. "I can re-tire now."

"Sue! I'm so sorry I didn't realize," he said. "Thirty years! We should have a party or something. Do you want to retire?"

Mrs. Brisbane sighed. "I'd miss Room Twenty-six ter-ribly. I'd miss all the wonderful students, especially Humphrey and Og. On the other hand, maybe it's time for someone else to have a chance. Am I really making a difference anymore?"

I had to squeak up. "YES-YES-YES!" I shouted. "You make a difference every day!"

"Humphrey seems to think so," Mr. Brisbane said. "And so do I."

"If I retired now, I'd be the one home alone all day." Mrs. Brisbane stood up. "I'm going to think about it a lit-tle longer."

What was there to think about? Sometimes Mrs. Brisbane could be quite frustrating. Sometimes Mrs. Bris-bane even made me a little bit mad. But always, Mrs. Brisbane was a really great teacher.

Bert spent the rest of the week making plans for his new job. He asked his wife if he could borrow me on the weekends once in a while.

"My students won't like it," she said. "But if you tell them it's for a good cause, they might not complain too much."

They didn't talk about the contract again for the rest of the week, so I spent many a long night spinning on my wheel and wondering what Mrs. Brisbane would decide.

❧

On our first day back at school, Principal Morales dropped by during recess. Mrs. Brisbane handed him the contract.

"I signed it," she said.

The principal smiled. "That's a great relief. What did Bert think?"

"Bert took a job and he can't wait to get out of the house," she said with a laugh. "It looks like neither of us are going to retire, at least this year."

I was so unsqueakably delighted, my heart went THUMP-THUMP-THUMP. Og was splashing so much, he practically created a tsunami in his tank, so I knew he was as happy as I was.

When my friends returned to the classroom, I watched them take their seats. I thought of how I'd seen Mrs. Brisbane help Sayeh, Garth, Gail and Heidi, Seth, Tabitha and Mandy—everyone in the class. Did they realize what she'd done for them?

I was afraid they didn't. I was GLAD-GLAD-GLAD Mrs. Brisbane was coming back. And I felt SAD-SAD-SAD that none of us appreciated her as much as we should.

REHABILITATION CENTER: A place where people who have been sick or injured go to rest and exercise so they can get strong again. This process works best when it involves a handsome, creative hamster.

Humphrey's Dictionary of Wonderful Words

15

Suggestions and Surprises

hat's what she said, Og," I told my froggy friend later that evening. "She wondered if she really made a difference."

"BOING-BOING!" He sounded truly alarmed.

"I know!" I answered. "No matter how much I try to tell her that everyone appreciates her, she doesn't understand."

"BOING-BOING-BOING!" At least Og seemed to get it.

"If there was just a way to get all her students together to thank her for all she's done! Boy, would she be surprised."

Og took a huge dive into his tank and splashed noisily.

I remembered what Mr. Brisbane told me on the way to Maycrest Manor. He said they were having a surprise party and I was the surprise.

"Og, we should give her a surprise party," I squeaked excitedly. I could just see it!

Og splashed like crazy. He wouldn't have any water left if he kept that up.

But how could a tiny hamster and a small frog manage to throw a party?

"*We* wouldn't have to give the party," I continued. "If we could just suggest it to somebody like Aldo, or a parent, or Principal Morales."

Og was silent. Maybe he was thinking. I was thinking, too. I was thinking that Mrs. Wright said that the principal had a suggestion box outside his office. If I could just put a suggestion in that box, maybe he would give a surprise party for Mrs. Brisbane.

I quickly told Og my idea. His response was quick. "BOING-BOING-BOING-BOING-BOING!"

"Great!" I answered. "All I have to do is write the suggestion and take it down to the office."

The fact that my tiny writing was hard for humans to read and the fact that I had no idea where the principal's office was did not discourage me one little bit.

Now I had a Plan.

I waited until Aldo had cleaned Room 26 before starting on the note. I neatly chewed a piece of paper from my notebook and took my small pencil. Then, in letters as big I could make them, I carefully wrote

Suggest: MRS. B.
30 YEARS
SURPRISE PARTY

Then I put the note in my mouth and opened the lock-that-doesn't-lock.

"Wish me luck, Oggy. I'm on my way!" I announced.

"BOING-BOING!" I knew that meant "good luck."

I then began the longest and most dangerous journey of my lifetime.

Of course, the door to Room 26 was shut. Aldo always closes and locks it when he leaves. How stupid of me not to think about it. I'm not one to give up easily, so I examined the bottom of the door and saw that there was a narrow opening. It wasn't much, but hamsters are able to flatten themselves and slip through some very small spaces, so it was worth a try.

Grasping the paper in my teeth, I hunkered down close to the floor and slid into the gap. I could feel the bottom of the door scraping my back, but I didn't mind because I'd made it!

It was dark out in the hallway and eerily quiet.

Now I faced another obstacle: which way was the principal's office? I figured it was near the front door, where I'd been carried in so many times. But the cage was always so thumpy and bumpy, it was hard to see where I was going.

I rushed past the side door to the playground—I certainly didn't want to go *there* at night—to the end of the corridor. There was some low light in the hall, which made it seem even creepier than if it had been completely dark. The doors here looked like other classrooms, except for a small door that had a sign reading Custodian over it. Aldo has his own room at Longfellow School? You learn something new every day!

I noticed something else: a sound was following me. *Crinkle-crinkle. Crinkle-crinkle.*

I stopped for a second and the sound stopped, too. I crept forward. *Crinkle-crinkle. Crinkle-crinkle.* The sound was back.

I stopped again and looked back over my shoulder. I didn't see anything: no Aldo, no aliens, nobody at all. When I turned back, the piece of paper I was holding in my teeth brushed against the floor. *Crinkle-crinkle-crinkle-crinkle.* Whew—that was the sound. I was following myself! I reminded myself to tell Og that part of the story when I got back. But first, I had to find the suggestion box.

I hurried down the hallway, glancing at each door. Then I looked straight ahead. There was the front door! And across from it was a big glass window and an even bigger door than the other rooms had. I moved closer and read the sign over the door: Principal.

JOY-JOY-JOY! I scurried as fast as I could toward that wonderful door. All I had to do was drop my note in the suggestion box and race back to Room 26 and my scheme would be a complete success.

Crinkle-crinkle-crinkle-crinkle. I looked up at that big door, but there was no box in front of the principal's office! Nothing next to it, either. It simply wasn't there. I stood there, feeling completely crushed.

And then, I looked straight up. There was a large box

attached to the door, way above my head. I backed up so I could read the writing on it: SUGGESTION BOX. That was great, but how was I supposed to get up there? I couldn't climb up the side of the doorway because it was completely smooth and there was nothing to hang on to. Even though I'm quite an acrobat, I certainly couldn't jump *that* high.

I remembered once when Richie and Seth made little airplanes by folding pieces of paper and throwing them. I wished I'd paid more attention. I considered making an airplane out of my suggestion, but I couldn't figure out how to sail it up to the box.

Just then, I heard the familiar squeaking of Aldo's cleaning cart. Normally, I was delighted to see my friend, but this time, I didn't want him to find me out of my cage. I dropped my suggestion on the floor and darted across the hall, into the shadows under a drinking fountain.

Aldo whistled a happy song as he pushed his cart past the drinking fountain. He didn't notice me, thank goodness. But he stopped in front of the principal's office and bent down to pick up the piece of paper. My heart sank when I saw him start to toss it into his trash bag. But then he stopped and examined it, lifting the note up so he could get more light.

"Mamma mia," he said. "Thirty years?" He looked puzzled. But instead of throwing the note in the trash, he dropped it in the suggestion box. Then he continued down the hall, turning right at the corner.

I heard another loud noise: THUMP-THUMP-THUMP. But I wasn't scared this time because I knew it was just the pounding of my heart.

I peeked around the corner just in time to see Aldo lock the door marked Custodian. He didn't have his cart anymore, so I guess he was finished for the night. He wore a hat now, and he turned and disappeared from view.

I counted to one hundred. When I was sure the coast was clear, I raced back down the hall and slid under the door of Room 26.

I had to swing back up to my table using the cord from the blinds like a trapeze, but I'd done that many times before. As scary as it was, it couldn't compare to what I'd experienced in the hallways of Longfellow School that night.

"BOING-BOING-BOING-BOING!" Og greeted me.

Once I was back in my cage, I took a long drink of water and caught my breath.

It took most of the rest of the night for me to tell Og all that had happened and for us both to ponder what Aldo thought about that note and whether Principal Morales would even read it.

I spent most of the next day dozing, but once or twice I woke up. I was pleased to see that Heidi was raising her hand, at least most of the time. When the last bell rang, Mrs. Brisbane quietly congratulated her and gave her a riddle sticker.

The rest of the week was QUIET-QUIET-QUIET. After all the testing, and the silliness, it was nice to be back to a normal classroom, but I was worried. Had Mr. Morales gotten the suggestion? Did he like the idea? And what would he do about it? In my time at Longfellow School, I've noticed that humans can be smart, nice and even important like the principal and still not understand the simplest thing a hamster tries to tell them.

You can have a great idea, you can have a Plan, but sometimes it doesn't work out. Maybe I could think of another way to tell Mrs. Brisbane what a great teacher she is, but for now, I was fresh out of ideas.

❧

Two weeks later, on a Friday afternoon, Mrs. Brisbane read aloud to us, which is something she does so well. This was a thumping good story about a pig. I've never seen a pig, but this story made me care about him a great deal. In fact, I was so nervous about what would happen to that pig, I hopped on my wheel for a good, fast spin.

Then it happened. That unbelievably loud BEEP-BEEP-BEEP was back and I was so surprised, I tumbled off my wheel into my soft bedding.

"Class, it's the fire alarm," said Mrs. Brisbane. She seemed a little nervous. "Please form two lines."

Even though Jeff Herman had said to leave the pets and let the firefighters rescue them, Garth and A.J. took Og's tank while Miranda gently picked up my cage. Sayeh came forward to help her.

"Children, no!" Mrs. Brisbane said.

"Please?" asked Miranda. We were already at the door.

Mrs. Brisbane shook her head. "Oh, go ahead."

Before I knew it, we were out in the hall, where all the other classes were lining up. In the distance, I heard the screech of Mrs. Wright's whistle.

And then we were outside. It was such a beautiful day! I was hoping there wasn't a real fire, not here or anywhere. But if there was, I was prepared to STOP-DROP-ROLL. As I looked around, I noticed that the playground looked a lot different than the last time we had a fire drill.

For one thing, there was a big, shiny fire engine parked near the swings. Sitting on top of the fire engine was our old friend Jeff Herman, smiling broadly. A small stage had been set up with a microphone. Sitting on the stage was none other than Mr. Brisbane, in his wheelchair. He was smiling, too. There were all kinds of familiar faces. Was that Aldo? And his wife, Maria? Many of my friends' parents were there. And some people who didn't seem to belong there at all, like Joyce from Maycrest Manor and Aldo's niece, Amy.

WHAT-WHAT-WHAT was going on? I wondered. And then I saw a banner draped above the stage. It said, MRS. BRISBANE APPRECIATION DAY.

I glanced over at my teacher. I've seen Mrs. Brisbane look happy, sad, mad, tired, puzzled and even discouraged. But I've never seen her look so surprised.

Mr. Morales stepped up onstage and tapped the microphone. "Ladies and gentlemen, students, we are gathered here to honor one of Longfellow School's greatest assets: Mrs. Sue Brisbane of Room Twenty-six. For thirty years, she's been informing, supporting and inspiring students in our community. And I think it's time that we all said, 'Thank you!'"

The crowd cheered wildly. "THANKS-THANKS-THANKS!" I shouted as loudly as my little lungs would let me. I heard an enthusiastic "BOING-BOING-BOING" behind me.

The principal continued. "As we all know, it's not easy to get Mrs. Brisbane out of her classroom, so I want to thank Jeff Herman of the Fire Department for helping us arrange this fire drill as part of our scheme. Thanks, Jeff."

After more applause, Mrs. Brisbane was called to the stage, where she took a seat next to Mr. Brisbane, who just couldn't stop smiling. Then, one by one, people came up to the microphone to thank Mrs. Brisbane. Aldo said she'd inspired him to go back to school to be a teacher. Amy said she'd inspired *her* to become a doctor. Joyce said Mrs. Brisbane had realized her son had a hearing problem and got him help. Other parents thanked her. And then, the students of Room 26 were called up to the stage.

Miranda brought me right along, and Richie and Kirk brought Og, too. Mrs. Wright stood in front of the stage and blew her whistle (of course). Garth started

strumming his guitar (where did that come from?).
Then my friends began to sing a song that sounded a lot
like "Yankee Doodle Came to Town," but with different words.

Mrs. Brisbane came to school
To teach us to be smarter,
When we tried to goof around,
She made us work much harder.

Mrs. Brisbane, keep it up,
You are oh so handy,
Keep on teaching kids like us,
And we will all be dandy.

Mrs. Brisbane taught us well,
Starting in September,
We have learned so much from her,
And we will all remember.

Mrs. Brisbane, thanks a lot,
We will not forget you,
Don't stop helping kids like us,
For we will never let you.

And then they all shouted, "Thanks, Mrs. Brisbane!"
Mr. Brisbane handed his wife a handkerchief and she
wiped her eyes. I wished I had a handkerchief, too.

Mr. Morales came to the microphone again and thanked Mrs. Wright. "It took some clever planning to keep this party and this song a surprise," he said. "Mrs. Wright taught the children the song during P.E. class. Our room mothers, Mrs. Hopper and Mrs. Patel, made a lot of calls, and our custodian, Aldo Amato, and his wife helped organize this day."

It was nice to think that Mr. Morales made a Plan, too. I always knew he was a very smart human.

Everyone applauded again. But Mr. Morales wasn't finished. "Most of the time, we don't thank our teachers until they retire. I'm so glad we had the chance to thank Mrs. Brisbane for *not* retiring. We hope she'll be here another thirty years."

"At least!" I squeaked, which made Miranda giggle.

"Finally, I can't take credit for thinking of this surprise party," Mr. Morales continued. "I have to thank an unknown person who left the suggestion in my suggestion box. Thank you, whoever you are."

"You're welcome," I squeaked softly.

~ ⋅◝◞⋅ ~

"So things worked out, Og," I said that evening when my friend and I were alone.

Og leaped up and dove down into his tank with a gigantic splash. That meant he was happy. So was I.

Sometimes you have to give a Plan a long time to work.

Sometimes things work out differently than you expected, but they still work out.

134

Life is full of surprises. And I think that's a VERY-VERY-VERY good thing.

SUGGESTION: An idea you offer to someone else in order to be helpful. It's a good idea to listen to suggestions, especially if they involve *parties* and, more importantly, if they involve parties honoring friends you REALLY-REALLY-REALLY like. If those parties include your favorite humans and nice speeches and some singing, so much the better.

Humphrey's Dictionary of Wonderful Words

Humphrey's Top Ten
Good Surprises

1. Share something with a friend: like ice cream (or broccoli—yum!) or a great book.

2. Put a note saying something nice about someone on his or her desk. Don't sign it! (And don't use the word *rat* in the note—NO-NO-NO! Unless you're talking about a pet rat you love. Because pet rats are almost as nice as hamsters.)

3. Throw a surprise party for someone special.

4. Help somebody (like your mom or dad or teacher) without being asked. Now *that's* a nice surprise!

5. Visit someone in the hospital or a retirement home. Bring something you can do together, like a puzzle or music to listen to.

6. Offer to read to your younger brothers and sisters. Or offer to play a game with them.

7. Draw a picture of someone you like and give it to that person.

8. Give your dog or cat (or hamster) a good scratching. They'll like it—but be gentle!

9. Smile at someone when they least expect it.

10. Invite a friend over to play with your hamster. FUN-FUN-FUN!

Dear Reader,

SURPRISE-SURPRISE-SURPRISE! Humphrey is back!

Since Humphrey loves adventures out of his cage so much, I thought it was high time he had his own hamster ball. That was a nice surprise for me to give him. But as I imagined him rolling across A.J.'s yard, I wondered what would happen if he rolled right up to a cat. That was a not-nice surprise for me to give him . . . but it was a lot of fun to write!

When readers ask me what happens to Humphrey in *Surprises According to Humphrey*, I tell them, "Well . . . he's very worried he might be abducted by aliens from another planet!" From the funny looks I get, I guess fans just can't figure out how that could be possible. I couldn't either, at first, but the dream about the alien carrots was one of the most fun sections of a Humphrey book I've ever written—at least until the next book.

After all, if I'm going to write a book to entertain readers, I'd better entertain myself as well. And I do. Whether I'm writing about rolling along in the hamster ball or dashing down to the Suggestion Box, I'm having *at least* as good a time as Humphrey.

But there are serious worries for Humphrey, too, as always. How can he help Garth and A.J. repair their friendship? How can he help inspire the people at Maycrest Manor? Will Mrs. Brisbane really retire? And how can one small hamster get a whole school to show appreciation for a great teacher?

Then there's the fire drill. No one really likes fire drills, except for the fact that they get people out of the classroom for a while. I don't think we take them very seriously. But knowing what to do in case of fire is as important for kids as it is for adults. I know, because my grandfather was a fireman with Engine Company 29. He saved many people's lives in days when firefighters didn't have the safety equipment that they have now. Grandpa's first name was Herman. We also have a fireman in the family now—my niece's husband. His first name is Jeff. So now you know how the firefighter Jeff Herman of Engine Company 29 came to be!

When my sister and I were little, it bothered Grandpa that we were a little *too* interested in matches. In those days, there were more matches around. You needed them in the kitchen to light the oven, and people smoked more, too. So one day, he sat us down at the kitchen table with matches and stood by watchfully as he made us light match after match after match until we were just plain sick of it! It worked, I guess, because I never played with matches after that.

Now, how to weave all these different threads—fire drills, hamster balls, aliens, and a cat—together into one story that somehow makes sense?

Like Humphrey, I usually start out with a Plan. But as in life, surprises pop up as I write.

It's funny to think that this is actually my job. How lucky can I be? And I consider myself especially lucky to be a F.O.H. (Friend of Humphrey).

I hope that you're a F.O.H., too!

From one friend to another,

Betty G. Birney

Meet Humphrey!

Everyone's favorite classroom pet!

Want more FUN–FUN–FUN?

Find fun Humphrey activities
and teachers' guides at
www.penguin.com/humphrey.

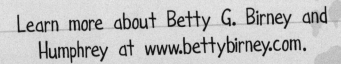

Learn more about Betty G. Birney and
Humphrey at www.bettybirney.com.

Welcome to Room 26, Humphrey!

You can learn a lot about life by observing another species. That's what Humphrey was told when he was first brought to Room 26. And boy, is it true! In addition to his classroom escapades, each weekend this amazing hamster gets to sleep over with a different student. Soon Humphrey learns to read, write, and even shoot rubber bands (only in self-defense). Humphrey's life would be perfect, if only the teacher weren't out to get him!

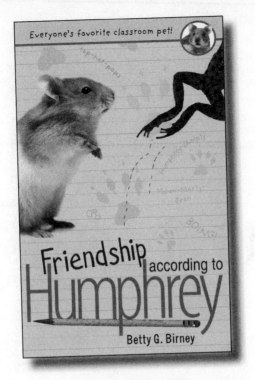

Everyone's favorite classroom pet!

Friendship according to Humphrey

Betty G. Birney

A New Friend?

Room 26 has a new class pet, Og the frog. Humphrey can't wait to be friends with Og, but Og doesn't seem interested. To make matters worse, the students are so fascinated by Og, they almost stop paying attention to Humphrey altogether! Humphrey knows that friendship can be tricky business, but if any hamster can become buddies with a frog, Humphrey can!

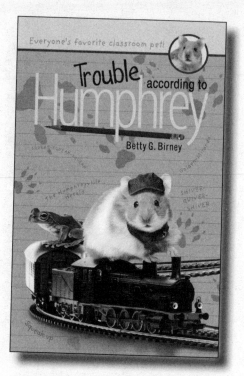

Humphrey to the Rescue!

Humphrey the hamster loves to solve problems for his classmates in Room 26, but he never meant to create one! Golden-Miranda, one of his favorite students, gets blamed when Humphrey is caught outside of his cage while she's in charge. Since no one knows about his lock-that-doesn't-lock, he can't exactly squeak up to defend her. Can Humphrey clear Miranda's name without giving up his freedom forever?

Everyone's favorite classroom pet!

Cats are SCARY-SCARY-SCARY.

April Fool!

Stop, Drop and Roll

I have a plan

Wacky Wednesday

Surprises according to Humphrey

Betty G. Birney

Surprises for Humphrey!

A classroom hamster has to be ready for anything, but suddenly there are LOTS-LOTS-LOTS of big surprises in Humphrey's world. Some are exciting, such as a new hamster ball. But some are scary, such as a run-in with a cat and a new janitor who might be from another planet. Even with all that's going on, Humphrey finds time to help his classmates with their problems. But will Mrs. Brisbane's unsqueakable surprise be too much for Humphrey to handle?

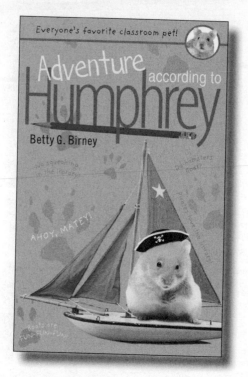

Adventure according to **Humphrey**

Betty G. Birney

Humphrey Sets Sail!

Humphrey's friends in Room 26 are learning about the ocean and boats, and Humphrey can't contain his excitement. He dreams about being a pirate on the high seas; and when the students build miniature boats to sail on Potter's Pond, Humphrey thinks he might get his wish. But trouble with the boats puts Humphrey in a sea of danger. Will Humphrey squeak his way out of the biggest adventure of his life?

Humphrey Is a Happy Camper!

When Humphrey hears that school is ending, he can't believe his ears. What's a classroom hamster to do if there's no more school? It turns out that Mrs. Brisbane has planned something thrilling for Humphrey and Og the frog: they're going to camp with Ms. Mac and lots of the kids from Room 26! Camp is full of FUN-FUN-FUN new experiences, but it's also a little scary. Humphrey is always curious about new adventures, but could camp be too wild even for him?

Everyone's favorite classroom pet!

School Days according to **Humphrey**

Betty G. Birney

Roll-Roll-Rolling-Rosie

It's the wrong room!

Rules of school

Hurry-Up-Harry

Pop-a wheelie!

Who Are These Kids?!

After an unsqueakably fun summer at camp, Humphrey can't wait to get back to Room 26 and see all of his classmates. But something fur-raising happens on the first day of school—some kids he's never seen before come into Mrs. Brisbane's room. And she doesn't even tell them they're in the wrong room! While Humphrey gets to know the new students, he wonders about his old friends. Where could they be? What could have happened to them?! It's a big mystery for a small hamster to solve. But as always, Humphrey will find a way!

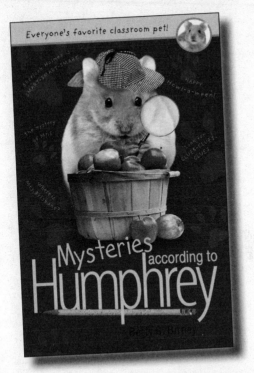

Mysteries according to Humphrey

EEK-EEK-EEK! Mrs. Brisbane Is Missing!

Humphrey has always investigated things, like why Speak-Up-Sayeh was so quiet and Tall-Paul and Small-Paul didn't get along, but this is a true mystery—Mrs. Brisbane is missing! She just didn't show up in Room 26 one morning and no one told Humphrey why. The class has a substitute teacher, called Mr. E., but he's no Mrs. Brisbane. Humphrey has just learned about Sherlock Holmes, so he vows to be just as SMART-SMART-SMART about collecting clues and following leads to solve the mystery of Mrs. Brisbane. . . .

Everyone's favorite classroom pet!

Winter according to Humphrey

Betty G. Birney

A Hamsterific Celebration of the Best Time of the Year!

Room 26 is abuzz. The students are making costumes and practicing their special songs for the Winter Wonderland program, and Humphrey is fascinated by all the ways his classmates celebrate the holidays (especially the yummy food). He also has problems to solve like how to get Do-It-Now-Daniel to stop procrastinating, convince Helpful-Holly to stop stressing over presents, and come up with the perfect gift for Og the frog. Of course he manages to do all that while adding delightful heart and humor to the holiday season.

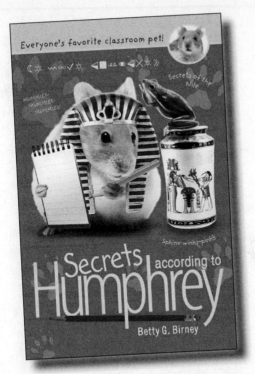

Everyone's favorite classroom pet!

Secrets of the Nile

MUMMIES-MUMMIES-MUMMIES!

Sphinx-winks-pinks

Secrets according to Humphrey

Betty G. Birney

Room 26 Is Full of Secrets, and Humphrey Doesn't Like It One Bit!

So many secrets are flying around Room 26 that Humphrey can barely keep track. Mrs. Brisbane knows a student is leaving, but Humphrey can't figure out which one. (Even more confusing, Mrs. Brisbane seems unsqueakably *happy* about it.) The class is studying the Ancient Egyptians, and some of the kids have made up secret clubs and secret codes. Even Aldo is holding back news from Humphrey.

Humphrey's job as classroom pet is to help his humans solve their problems, but all these secrets are making it HARD-HARD-HARD!

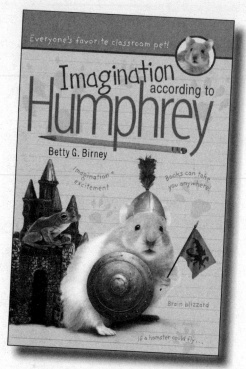

On the book cover:

Everyone's favorite classroom pet!

Imagination according to
Humphrey

Betty G. Birney

Imagination = excitement

Books can take you anywhere!

Brain blizzard

If a hamster could fly...

Even a Little Hamster
Can Have a Big Imagination!

Imaginations are running wild in Mrs. Brisbane's class, but Humphrey is stumped. His friends are writing about where they would go if they could fly, but Humphrey is HAPPY-HAPPY-HAPPY right where he is in Room 26. It's pawsitively easy for Humphrey to picture exciting adventures with dragons and knights in the story Mrs. Brisbane is reading aloud. If only his imagination wouldn't disappear when he tries to write. Luckily, Humphrey likes a challenge, and Mrs. Brisbane has lots of writing tips that do the trick.

WATCH OUT FOR HUMPHREY'S BOOK OF UNSQUEAKABLY FUN JOKES AND PUZZLES!

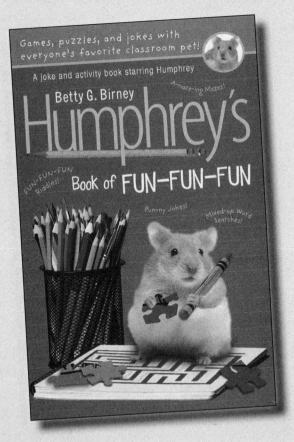

IF YOU LIKE PETS AND ANIMALS,
BE SURE TO PICK UP HUMPHREY'S
BOOK OF PET FACTS AND TIPS!

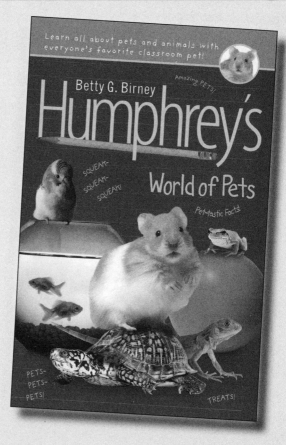